FRY & LAURIE

BIT NO. 4

Stephen Fry and Hugh Laurie are both writers, comedians and actors. They met at university, where they co-wrote and appeared in the embarrassingly-titled *The Cellar Tapes*, which won the Perrier Award at the Edinburgh Fringe in 1981. They have since worked together on a number of things, including *Alfresco, Friday Night Live* and *Saturday Live, Blackadder, Jeeves and Wooster*, and four series of *A Bit of Fry & Laurie* for the BBC. Stephen Fry has also written two novels, *The Liar* and *The Hippopotamus*, and Hugh has read them. They are both capable of making conversation, should the need arise.

STEPHEN FRY and HUGH LAURIE

FRY&LAURIE

BIT NO. 4

Mandarin

This book is dedicated to Michael Atherton

A Mandarin Paperback
FRY & LAURIE – BIT No.4

First published in Great Britain 1995
by Mandarin Paperbacks
an imprint of Reed Consumer Books Ltd
Michelin House, 81 Fulham Road, London SW3 6RB
and Auckland, Melbourne, Singapore and Toronto

Stills from *A Bit of Fry and Laurie*, a
BBC Television Production, produced by
Jon Plowman, directed by Bob Spiers
Photographs copyright © BBC 1995

A CIP catalogue record for this title
is available from the British Library
ISBN 0 7493 1967 4

Printed and bound in Great Britain
by Clays Ltd, St Ives plc

The authors would like to highlight a raft of key thanks towards
Jon Plowman and Bob Spiers, who produced and directed
the fourth series of *A Bit of Fry & Laurie*. They were, on the whole,
punctual, polite, and smartly dressed. Their contribution was
never unwelcome, and occasionally insightful.

S.F. & H.L.
Zum Wilden Hirsch, Bavaria
October 1994

Messrs Fry (Stephen) and Laurie (Hugh) would like to make it plain to Mr Public (Joe), Mrs Public (Josephine), Master Public (Joey), Miss Public (Joannettella), Ms Public (Jonquil) and Lord Public (Jodhpur) that the frail barque that is *A Bit of Fry & Laurie* could never have slipped gracefully into the waters of televisual transmission without the assistance of a team of dedicated, highly trained, highly motivated, highly flexible and highly paid professionals.

They (the Fry and the Laurie mentioned upstairs in the attic-level paragraph) draw the attention of the Public family to the following key Guest Personnel, whose talent, charm, beauty, patience, creative genius and sheer bloody guts, intestinal gristle and bowel helped pull the whole thing through. Their names have been listed according to the following algorithm: let the string 'L$' equal the first letter of guest n's surname and let 'M$' equal the second letter etc. Let 'Ln' equal x, where the variable x is calculated against a table in which the alphanumeric 'A' of the alphabet equals 1 and the letter Z equals 26. Let a shell-sort then loop through the surnames assigning values and listing the resultant guest names such that those with the lowest value appear before those with the highest. In a sense, one might say therefore, that the following list appears in alphabetical order.

> Barlow, Patrick
> Bird, John
> Booker, Jane
> Dawes, Robert
> Duvitski, Janine
> Gillies, Fiona
> Law, Phyllida
> Macnally, Kevin
> Mantle, Clive
> Moore, Stephen
> Quentin, Caroline
> Staunton, Imelda

Those listed above are good people, stout people, fine people. If they had not kindly consented to be guests, well, we would have had to find some other people. We love them, we reverence them, we thank them, we acknowledge them and everybody who knows them.

Contents

Introduction ix
Grey and Hopeless 1
Sexual Relations 3
Smell 5
Blame 7
Charter 10
Channel Changer 12
Kitchen 14
Wonderful Life 16
Dog Hamper 20
Child Abuse 21
Young Tory of the Year 22
Interrogation 24
Avenger 27
Going for Gold 29
Gossiping Heads 30
Fascion 32
Operational Criteria 34
Fan Club 37
The Duke of Northampton 39
A.I. 43
Real Reality 46
Barman 48
Karaoke 50
Sophisticated Song 52
For Some Reason Angry 53

Cigars 54
Don't be Dirty 57
Interruptus 60
Soccer School 63
Golf 66
Head Gardener 70
Red and Shiny 72
Dalliard: Piano 73
Gelliant Gutfright 77
Grand Prix 82
Tribunal 83
Honda 85
Pooch 87
Disgusting 89
Dalliard: Models 90
Oprah Winfrey 94
Religianto 96
Consent 99
Truancy 103
Death Threat 105
All We Gotta Do 106
Fast Monologue 107
Stapler 109
Time Complaint 112
Cocktails 114

Introduction

Stephen	Hugh, my old china serving bowl, it seems that we're pretty much in the position of having to say 'Here we are again.'
Hugh	Stephen, my old styrofoam cushion whose wedge-shape guarantees relief from the misery of lower back pain, you've never said a truer word.
Stephen	We sit here, do we not, like coiled springs, gazing down the comedy tunnel ahead of us, settling our spikes into the starting blocks and cocking our ears to the starter's pistol. Before us, the hurdles and water-jumps of three and a half hours' worth of comedy material, the first forty minutes to be run in lanes – ecstasy, pain, triumph, disaster, who knows what awaits at the further end?
Hugh	My hope is that, win or lose, at least there'll be a steaming mug of hot Lucozade, and maybe one of those aluminium blankets of the sort that help prevent athletes from not wearing aluminium blankets.
Stephen	Hugh, as always, your words fill me with a ferocious desire to be somewhere else.
Hugh	Well, violent reader, as I'm by way of being the person to the left of the dealer, it falls to me to welcome you to this book or...
Stephen	Yes?
Hugh	... this book or...

Hugh thinks for a moment, tilting his head to the light in a way that might remind the casual onlooker of a young Arthur Mullard.

	There's no other word for 'book', really, is there?
Stephen	Not one that need detain us for more than the fewest of moments, Hugh, no.
Hugh	So welcome to this book. And let me begin by saying, don't read it straight away.
Stephen	A strange piece of advice, old friend, and yet...

Stephen pauses, tilting his head to the light in a way that might remind a young Arthur Mullard of an old Trevor Francis.

Hugh	And yet?
Stephen	And yet I've ridden too far with you, known you too long, been at your side in too many tight corners not to doubt that you have your reasons.
Hugh	My reasons are almost painfully simple.
Stephen	I suspected they might be.

Hugh	This book is more than it appears.
Stephen	You mean less, surely?
Hugh	I mean more, dammit. Much, much more. It contains traps, conceits, windows on to other worlds, and almost no crosswords. I advise you to lay on its side in the middle of your living-room floor and walk around it, sniffing, probing, prodding. But whatever you do . . . *never turn your back on it.*
Stephen	Even for a second.
Hugh	Even, as you so rightly point out, for a second.
Stephen	I'd like to add something at this point.
Hugh	Let me suggest seventeen and twelve.
Stephen	*(after some thought)* Twenty-nine.
Hugh	Good. But to return to the matter in hand. Books, I always like to shout, can be divided into two categ. . .
Stephen	I don't do dividing.
Hugh	Ng . . . into two categories. Books for reading and books for skimming, dipping and grazing.
Stephen	That's beautiful. That is actually beautiful.
Hugh	I think it fair to say that this book, our book, falls heavily and with a sickening thud, jarring the table and spilling some of that very nice medium dry sherry, into the second category.
Stephen	Correct.
Hugh	And we're proud of that. That's not to take anything away from the first categ. . .
Stephen	I don't do taking away either.
Hugh	Hng . . . I suppose what I'm trying to say is this . . . here, let me show you . . .

Hugh mimes what he is driving at . . . rather well.

Stephen	Exactly! That's absolutely right. That, above all, is the point we wanted to drive home, snog briefly in the porch and then take upstairs for a rough round of banal sex.
Hugh	Banal sex?
Stephen	Bexactly.

Hugh and Stephen break off for a moment, tilting a pair of Arthur Mullards towards the light in a way that reminds them of what has to be said next.

Hugh	I've got it. There's the old warning song, isn't there?
Stephen	Of course! That's it! How could you have been so stupid?
Hugh	I don't know. I really don't.
Stephen	Well get on with it. The ladies and gentlemen are waiting. . .

Hugh	It goes like this. One afternoon, while I was out brushing my teeth, I met a man called Palfrey, who claimed to be our legal adviser from the legal department, specifically the section that deals with legal matters and issues pertaining to the whole business of the law. He legally advised me that I should advise you, the reader, if that is what you are, that the public performance of any of the material herewithcontained without the written permission of the authors or their duly appointed agents, shall not be deemed . . .

There is a pause. Not so long as to arouse comment, but let's face it, we've all known shorter ones.

Stephen	Not be deemed . . .?
Hugh	I don't know. I don't suppose I shall ever know what it will not be deemed.
Stephen	You mean . . .?
Hugh	Exactly. At that moment, a white Nissan Sunny, its tyres howling in protest, rounded the corner and careered towards Palfrey. I made to shout a warning, but, for some reasons I will never understand, the words froze in my throat. I could only stand and watch in horror as the bonnet of the car struck Palfrey behind the knees, sending the little lawyer's body arching through the air in a bizarre arabesque of death.
Stephen	Did you call Nick Ross?
Hugh	Of course. But for Palfrey, it was a lifetime too late.
Stephen	What a ghastly story.
Hugh	I know.
Stephen	And so badly told.
Hugh	You're quite right.
Stephen	Well heigh ho. The time has come for us to take up a bottle of Sainsbury's cooking champagne and smash it over the bows of this book . . .
Hugh	. . . then watch in triumph as it slithers down the ramp into the oily waters of the reader's shopping bag . . .
Stephen	Or back on to the shelf, as the case may be . . .
Hugh	Allowing them to maunder along to another of the million or so comedy books currently on sale . . .
Stephen	In whichever category you place yourself, may you find whatever it is you're looking for . . .
Hugh	And may it come up to expectations when you do . . .
Stephen	We love you . . .
Hugh	. . . love you . . .
Stephen	. . . love you . . .
Hugh	. . . love you . . .

Stephen and Hugh grow fainter and fainter, until they have to sit down.

Grey and Hopeless

Hugh is sitting at his desk in his office. Stephen, his boss, comes in.

Stephen   Ah, Douglas, those reports were supposed to be on my desk yester...

He notices that Hugh is looking signally depressed.

    ...you all right, Douglas?

Hugh   I'm sorry sir, I just ... it's just ...

Stephen   Come on, old fellow, spit it out. Whatever it is, it can't be that bad.

Hugh   I've got this feeling that my life is grey and hopeless.

Stephen   Grey and hopeless? Grey and hopeless? Oh now, come on. What are you talking about?

Hugh   I look into the future and what do I see?

Stephen   I don't know, what do you see?

Hugh   Just the blank rolling of the years, one after another, like grey, hopeless waves beating against my brains till the blood runs out of my ears.

Stephen   Now come on. You've got a wife and two children, a very pleasant house, three loving goldfish ...

Hugh   I know, but what does it mean? We live in a doomed world. Doomed.

Stephen   Oh nonsense, what do you mean doomed?

Hugh   Nobody likes anybody any more, nobody cares about anybody or anything. People go around hitting and stabbing and stealing and insulting. The countryside's a poisonous mess, the cities are unbreathable, you can get beaten up by a twelve-year-old and ripped off by your neighbour.

Stephen   Well, I grant you things aren't ...

Hugh   There are no certainties, only battle-lines. No pleasure any more except in getting drunk or high on dangerous drugs that are supplied by maniacs with machine guns.

Stephen   Yes, it's a grim old world alright, but surely it's always been ...

Hugh   Films and music are crap. Books are crap. The streets are so full you can't walk in a town without being pushed off the pavement, the roads are unusable, the trains are a joke, the politicians are so feeble-minded and gutless you can't even hate them.

Stephen   Even sport isn't fun any more, really, is it?

Hugh   You smile at someone in the street, you're either knifed in the kidneys or in court for rape.

Stephen   Opening a newspaper's like opening a fold of used lavatory paper.

Hugh   Turn on the television and you're sprayed in coloured vomit.

Stephen   It's frigging useless, isn't it?

Hugh   We're done for.

Stephen	Shagged. We're bloody shagged. Oh, Jesus.
Hugh	Grey and hopeless.
Stephen	Grey and hopeless.
Hugh	Just a nightmare of cold despair.
Stephen	No future, no point, no prospect, no pleasure, nothing. Just grey, hopeless hell.
Hugh	Christ.
Stephen	Oh Christ Jesus.
Hugh	We're dead.

Pause: an incredibly long one. Then they turn to the camera.

Stephen	Well, first of all, m'colleague and I would like to welcome you to this brand new spanking series of *A Bit of Fry & Laurie*, the show that tries to bring a little jolliness into the darker corners of modern Britain, but doesn't.
Hugh	I'd like to add my own individual welcome on a more personal note, separate and distinct from m'colleague's joint welcome, which I always think is a bit stiff, a bit formal. My welcome is just a bit of an old 'Hi'. That's all. Just 'Hi.'
Stephen	Jesus. So a choice of welcomes on BBC television. It's either good evening, ladies and gentlemen, or it's . . .
Hugh	Hi.

VOX POP **Hugh** Well, you see, you take away the Queen, I mean, it's all very well to say, get rid of the Royal family, but – who the hell are you going to put on the stamps? Hm? Desmond Lynam? Mike Smith? I mean, I'm not going to turn Mike Smith over and give him a licking every time I want to send a letter, am I? People just don't think these things through.

Sexual Relations

Stephen   I haven't enjoyed sexual relations with my wife now for seven or eight years. We still make love every night, it's just that I don't enjoy it. Well, that's not good enough, so I decided to do something about it.

He walks down a corridor.

After all, how much do we really know about love-making? We all think we know, don't we? Well, perhaps you'd be surprised. Dr Hedges Evan is a sex therapist. He also, I'm told, makes the best cup of coffee in North London. Let's find out.

We're now outside a door. 'Dr Hedges Evan'.
Cut to interior of office. Hugh is Hedges Evan.

Hugh   The first thing I always say is this. Don't be afraid to experiment and above all don't be afraid to talk things through. To do it well takes time. If you're using the drip method, then make sure that everything is properly wiped down first.

Stephen   *(sipping from a cup)* Well the results speak for themselves.

Hugh   You're very tall.

Stephen   No, no. I mean it.

Hugh   Well, thank you.

Stephen   Would you say that most couples would benefit from sex therapy, Dr Evan?

Hugh   I have a handy little memory-aid to help describe the problems that confront most couples. They are the enemies of good sex and I refer to them as the two F's, the I, the N, the T and the other F. The two F's are Fear and Inhibition, the I is Myth and Fallacy, the T is Silence and the other F is Worry.

Stephen   Right . . .

Hugh   And the most important of those F's is Ignorance. For instance most people are surprisingly ill-informed about the absolute basics, the one, B, C's of sex, if you like.

Stephen   Now that's a very interesting point, Doctor.

Hugh   Thanks.

Stephen   What are some of the most common mistakes, would you say?

Hugh   Well, I'll give you a for-instance. I had a couple in here not so very long ago, a news-reader and his wife as it happens, although it could just as easily have been a wife and her news-reader, and they had come to me complaining that their love life wasn't really working out. And do you know what the poor man had been trying to do?

Stephen Of course I don't.

Hugh I mean, I hear some pretty hair-raising stories in this office, as you can imagine, but that absolutely took the biscuit. He'd been trying to push his penis into his poor wife's vagina.

Stephen And that's bad, is it?

Hugh Well, I mean the idea is grotesque. I can't afford to be moralistic or a prude in my job, but I can tell you, I very nearly threw up.

Stephen Mm...

Hugh Ignorance, you see. With a capital W.

Stephen So what did you do?

Hugh I sat them down, first of all.

Stephen They'd been standing up through all of this?

Hugh No, I had sat them down to begin with, but then they stood up to show me a couple of things...

Stephen Gotcha.

Hugh And I turned round to them, and I said...

Stephen You turned round to them, so you were facing...?

Hugh That wall there.

Stephen I have a clear picture now.

Hugh And I talked for nearly twenty minutes...

Stephen Did you check your watch?

Hugh I don't wear a watch. I find it makes me rash.

Stephen I see.

Hugh No, I went by the clock above the main entrance.

Stephen So while you were talking, you weren't actually in the room with them?

Hugh I find it works for me.

Stephen And what was the result of all this? Satisfied customers?

Hugh They are now happily divorced, I'm pleased to say.

Stephen Both of them?

Hugh Both of them, indeed. The news-reader's career seems to go from strength to strength, and his wife is now the President of France.

Stephen Oh good. No chance of another cup, is there?

Hugh Every chance in Christendom.

Smell

Stephen talks. John is at his side.

Stephen We see things. We touch things. We hear things. We taste things. But never forget that we also smell.

Huge caption: 'SMELL – THE FORGOTTEN SENSE?'

John, my spies tell me, and I should point out that they're not really spies in the sense of having hidden cameras and false bottoms, they're just people who tell me things – my spies tell me that, in your spare time, you're Vice-Professor of Smell at De Montfort University – reserve your seat of learning – do you think we've forgotten smell?

John I think we have forgotten smell. I think we neglect smell. I think smell is the one sense that seems to have got left behind in the mad rush for profit and cheap housing.

Stephen Can you give us some examples?

John Of what?

Stephen Anything.

John Alright. First leg qualifier against Holland. Libby Purves. Beethoven's Violin Concerto.

Stephen They being examples of . . .?

John Of the glaring deficiencies of the long ball game, a Radio Four presenter, and a violin concerto by Beethoven.

Stephen But to get back to this wretched business of smell . . .

John Well now, I have to pick you up on that. I can't let that go unchallenged.

Stephen waits, but there is no more.

Stephen Fair enough. I believe you've actually brought some smells with you, to give us some idea of the kind of thing *you* say, and I stress the you, when I say *you* say, that we're missing.

John rummages at his feet and brings out some bottles.

John That's right. Have a go at this one, and tell me what you think.

Stephen takes the bottle and sniffs.

Stephen Hmm. Pretty nasty. What is that?

John That one is . . .

He looks at the label.

... Michael Portillo getting out of a Rover 200 after quite a long journey.

He hands over another bottle.

Stephen	Ah now, that's rather nice.
John	'Tis, isn't it? That's the inside of a slaughterhouse in Kent. Fresh, tangy, but full of character.

Another bottle.

Stephen	Hello. I think I recognise this one.
John	You should do ...
Stephen	What is it?
John	Have a guess.
Stephen	Well I don't know ...
John	Go on ...
Stephen	The lavatories at Earls Court during the Royal Tournament?
John	No. That's actually your right knee.
Stephen	Is it?

Stephen smells his own knee.

Stephen	Good heavens, so it is.
John	There you are, you see.
Stephen	And *you* say, *you* say, that a lot of ordinary people are missing out on this sense.
John	*I* say that. *I* say that. And I think that's a shame.
Stephen	So do I.

VOX POP **Hugh** No I love this country. I do, I love it. Only trouble is there's nowhere to park, is there?

Blame

Jane gets back home. She comes into the sitting-room, and screams. Pan across to find Hugh with a blood-soaked knife, standing over the bodies of an elderly couple.

Jane	Oh my God ... what's happened? Victor ...?
Hugh	I am bloody furious, Jennifer, I don't mind telling you.
Jane	The blood ... what's happened?
Hugh	What's happened? I've killed your parents, that's basically what's happened.
Jane	What?
Hugh	Stabbed them both to death.
Jane	What ...?
Hugh	I could not be more furious.
Jane	Stabbed ... but why?
Hugh	Exactly. Why? It was so unnecessary. That's why I'm so bloody annoyed.
Jane	What ...?
Hugh	Your father was being a bit ratty, complained that the tonic water was flat, and suddenly I was stabbing him in the neck with a knife. I mean, what is going on here?
Jane	You killed him?
Hugh	Yeah, alright, don't go on about it. I mean how do you think I feel?
Jane	I don't know, Victor ...
Hugh	Bloody annoyed, that's how.
Jane	Annoyed?
Hugh	Somebody should have stopped this ...
Jane	But I had to go out ...
Hugh	No, no, I'm not blaming you, darling. Somebody. Police, social services. Somebody should have seen that this was a tragedy waiting to happen and done something about it. I really am livid.
Jane	What about mother?
Hugh	Well, she got in the way, tried to defend him, and suddenly she was lying there, dead, the victim of bureaucratic inefficiency. It just won't do.
Jane	Have you called the police?
Hugh	Well, no. I thought I'd write, actually. I think it would have more weight.
Jane	No, I mean, have you told them what you've done?
Hugh	What *I've* done?
Jane	Yes ...
Hugh	What *I've* done. Oh that's nice. That's really charming. I stab your parents to death with a bread knife, and suddenly it's my fault, is it?

7

Jane	But Victor, darling, you did it. You said so yourself...
Hugh	My hand did it, Jennifer. My hand and the knife did it, yes. But what made my hand do it? That's what you should be asking yourself.
Jane	Well, *you*...
Hugh	No. Absolutely not. It's the system. I loved your parents, Jennifer. You know that. Your father sometimes smelt a bit, but they were lovely people, and now they're dead. All because the system failed. Again.
Jane	You're right. I shouldn't have left you alone. It's all my fault.
Hugh	Well, that was my first reaction, I must admit. Bloody Jennifer, I thought, left me in a right pickle, but it's not you, darling. There are people paid to make sure this doesn't happen, and those people simply didn't do their job.
Jane	But if I'd been here...
Hugh	But you weren't, my angel. The system failed you, just like it failed me.
Jane	What are we going to do now?
Hugh	Well, I've got a good mind to kill you, to be honest.
Jane	Me?
Hugh	Teach the bloody social services a lesson. See if they can talk their way out of three dead bodies. I'd like to see them try...
Jane	Well, I'd rather you didn't.
Hugh	Well, of course *I'd* rather I didn't. But my hand, Jennifer. What is making my hand do these things?
Jane	The system.

The doorbell goes. Jane goes to answer it.

Hugh	Thank you. The bloody system. These people, with their fat bloody salaries, sitting in their cosy little offices while your parents, Jennifer, good people, honest, decent people, are being slaughtered. What is this country coming to?

Jane comes back in with John.

John	Mr Hammond?
Hugh	Yes?
John	Derek Broome, Social Services.
Hugh	Oh, well, there you go. Hurrah for the bloody cavalry. I hope you're satisfied...
John	I'm sorry?
Jane	Victor's killed my parents. Stabbed them with a knife.
John	Oh damn.
Hugh	Oh damn, yes, well, that's not a lot of use, is it? What have you got to say for yourself?

John	Well you were down on my list, Mr Hammond, of tragedies waiting to happen, but I got held up.
Hugh	You hear that, Jennifer? Mr Broome 'got held up'. Jesus.
John	If you'd accept my department's apologies, Mr Hammond, for the inconvenience this has caused you and your wife, and I'll see if I can't arrange a complimentary food hamper to be delivered here without delay.
Hugh	Well, that's something.
Jane	It's not much good to my parents, though, is it?
Hugh	Well said, Jennifer. Bloody well said.
John	Well, how about this? These vouchers *(hands over some slips of paper)* entitle you to dinner for two at the Laudanum Hotel, plus five years' bereavement counselling absolutely free.
Jane	Hmm.
Hugh	Well. That's more like it.

VOX POP Stephen Memory can play the weirdest tricks on you. It really can. I remembered something the other day, just as I was leaving the house, I turned round to lock the back door, and I remembered that I'd been violently abused as a child for nearly twelve years. Just came from nowhere. Amazing. I'm suing my parents for five million quid, as it happens. Course they died some years back, so I've got to sue myself as next of kin, but I think the principle's important.

Charter

Stephen addresses the camera.

Stephen	Yes. Quite funny. But only quite.
Hugh	*(off)* Thanks very much.
Stephen	But what can you do about it? Until recently, nothing. But ladies, and in a broader sense, gentlemen, m'colleague and I, concerned as ever with a relentless drive for higher standards, have decided to institute a Charter. A Charter that guarantees you the very highest standard of comic service.

Hugh has joined Stephen.

Hugh	The Charter, or Charter, that we are proposing contains a raft of key points, a key basket of top proposals and a top key package of key top measures, to ensure that you, the viewer ...
Stephen	The customer ...
Hugh	The client ...
Stephen	The punter or puntress ...
Hugh	The John or Jane Doe ...
Stephen	The Fred or Frederica Bloggs ...
Hugh	The man ...
Stephen	Or ladygirl ...
Hugh	The man or ladygirl who would have been on the Clapham omnibus, but discovered after waiting for two hours that it's been cancelled and replaced by a bright yellow transit van that only runs at peak times ...
Stephen	... whenever the bleeding hell they are ...
Hugh	To ensure that you have the right, the muscle, the arse-widening power, to MAKE A DIFFERENCE.
Stephen	There are two main prongs ...
Hugh	By which we mean two main sticky-out bits at the end.
Stephen	There is quality and there is delivery.
Hugh	Any joke which fails to come up to the normally high, rigorous, ruthless standards you would expect of *A Bit of Fry & Laurie* can be reported to the Charter Commission where it will be inspected by a top team of key experts, who will then pass it on to a key team of top experts.
Stephen	If your complaint is upheld the joke will be humanely destroyed.
Hugh	Which brings us to our other sticky-out bit. Delivery.
Stephen	Prong two. Delivery. In a modern society, jokes *must* be delivered on time: if you experience any delivery where the timing is too ...

Hugh	. . . slow.
Stephen	Or if the . . .
Hugh	*(interrupting)* Quick.
Stephen	. . . timing should be . . .
Hugh	Or if the joke simply never even . . .

Pause.

Stephen	The Commission will be only too happy to look into it. The Comedy Charter: peace of mind. Audience power. Your guarantee of service and quality . . . without dripping.
Hugh	Anyway. On with the ruthless subversion of family values . . .

VOX POP

Hugh You know that Kevin Major? Well, I'd have to say that he's one of the most consistently impressive, dignified, articulate and rousing speakers I've ever heard.

Stephen's voice off.

Stephen Thank you very much. And now could you give us an example of sarcasm?

Hugh Well it's almost the same, isn't it?

Channel Changer

An advertisement: the kind we get for didi-seven that they show in the afternoons.

Stephen is lounging in a chair watching television. Newman and Baddiel comes on, so he decides to change channels. He looks around the sofa for his channel changer.

John   *(voice-over)* Can't find that channel changer?

Stephen digs a hand behind the sofa.

Where did I put it last? Is this always happening to you? Sometimes actually have to get up to find it?

Stephen raises his massive wobbling bulk off the sofa and looks under a pile of satellite magazines.

All those channels available in authentic cinema sound, plus laserdisc, CD-I, game gear, video, satellite, home-shopping . . . but no use without a channel changer.

Stephen really irritated.

But who wants to get up and find it? Now there's the amazing Wristchanger.

Stephen sits in front of TV, slumped in chair holding a Wristchanger.

Available in a choice of one arresting colours and fabrics, the Wristchanger simply locks on to your wrist . . .

Stephen snaps it on to his wrist.

. . . and need never be lost again. No more digging behind sofas, no more unnecessary and unpleasant standing up. Change channels with maximum comfort to all muscle groups.

Stephen happily sorts through thousands of channels.

But that isn't all. As an introductory offer to the Wristchanger, we're offering two more items designed to enhance viewer comfort.

Stephen's knee begins to jog up and down.

You know that feeling. You're settled in to your favourite American wrestling programme and suddenly ... Ow! Nature calls.

Stephen reaches for an old milk bottle.

Well now you can say goodbye to old milk bottles or the more distressing effort associated with standing up. Introducing Comfipee.

Cutaway to strange item that might well be used by astronauts.

Plumbed into your home, Comfipee allows you to expel those wastes that build up in the bladder after a hard afternoon's drinking of your favourite diet cola or isotonic drink (because sure, fitness is important) without having to leave the action.

Stephen, watching, and obviously enjoying a good pee at the same time. A warm smile spreads over his face as he releases.

But it doesn't stop there, because Comfipee comes with a completely free companion ... Comfipoo.

Cutaway to an even stranger contraption.

We know what those pizzas turn into inside your tummy. Before, you used to have to get up to do something about it. No longer. Comfipoo to the rescue.

Stephen, watching TV and clearly enjoying a good crap.

Comfipoo's built-in wiper, moist-wipe and talcum module gives you total freshness. Comfipee and Comfipoo ... real convenience. Remember, Wristchanger, Comfipee and Comfipoo are not available in the shops. Have your credit card handy while we tell you about the total eat, sleep, shop system you can enjoy. The Cradle to Grave In-Sofa Stayathome System.

Stephen, with food dispenser attached to him.

With the total viewing Stayathome System you need never get up out of that chair again ... guaranteed! You order your food and your new decoders and videos through home shopping, you enjoy them all in-sofa. From cradle to grave, a world of entertainment just for you.

Kitchen

John is at a kitchen counter in the studio. Stephen is at his side.

Stephen   But less of that earlier. John, you've been looking forward to the summer salad season, I believe.

John   I certainly have, Chris. A lot of supermarkets these days package fresh herbs. I'm particularly fond of this one here.

Lifts a pinch of some green dried herb from a small bowl.

Stephen   Delicious, I must say. Dill?

John   Well, no and that's the point.

Stephen   It is?

John   It is. But I've found this very handy way of preparing it. The usual problem is one of wet lips rotting away the paper.

Stephen   Hello.

John   But if you take an ordinary Rizzla packet like this.

Brings out Rizzla packet.

Stephen   Woah.

John   You can simply tear the strip off here and use it to form a protective cardboard roach. That way the herb . . .

Stephen   *(hastily)* Let's see what Jane and Frank are up to over there.

Cut to Hugh and Jane.

Hugh   Well, here we are, with Jane's blind taste test. Ready, Jane?

Jane has a blindfold on.

Jane   As I'll ever be.

Hugh screams with laughter.

Hugh   As I'll ever be, dear oh dear . . .

Jane sips at a glass of red wine.

Any thoughts at all, Jane?

Jane   Wine?

Huge applause.

Hugh	Incredible. Can you name the colour?
Jane	White.
Hugh	Oh ... Very nearly. Very nearly indeed. Have another go ...
Jane	Well ...
Hugh	Go on, one more go. I'm sure you'll get it this time ...
Jane	Blue?
Hugh	Nggg ...
Jane	I know! It's red. Definitely red.

Huge applause.

Hugh   Jane, that is remarkable. Have a go at this one.

Hands her another glass – she sips.

Thoughts?

Jane	Oh I know this one. It's a Pomerol.
Hugh	Yes ...
Jane	... late growth '89, Manon des Haut Louvarges ...
Hugh	Extraordinary ...
Jane	... from the north side of the hill ...
Hugh	North it is ...
Jane	... £8.85 ...
Hugh	... yes ...
Jane	... opened with an air-injection cork pull ...
Hugh	... yes ...
Jane	... poured out by a middle-aged man with cream-coloured trousers, who lives in Putney ...
Hugh	*(calls)* Tony?
Voice off	Mortlake.
Hugh	Mortlake, but near enough. Anything else?
Jane	... thirty-three to one outsider Saffron Lad will win the National by eight lengths, there will be a mild earthquake in Mexico City at the end of August, the Liberal Democrats will take South Molesey with a thirty per cent swing, and Frank ...
Hugh	Still here, my darling ...
Jane	You should beware of anyone called Rupert ...
Hugh	Will do ...
Jane	And electric fans.
Hugh	Rupert and electric fans, gotcha.

Wonderful Life

Rolling violins. Hugh is standing at a bridge in the snow, red-eyed, hopeless waves of despair rolling and breaking over him. He is unshaven and a trail of blood comes from his lip. He stares into the swirling waters below, shaking his head. He has an Australian accent.

Hugh It's over. It's all over. Just end it. The whole bloody thing's gone, finished, over with. Face it, the world would be a better place without you. I should never have been born. Oh, Jesus.

He bites his knuckle in despair. Stephen approaches him in the background. Hugh climbs over the bridge.

Stephen Don't do it, son. Oh my.

Splosh! Hugh has jumped in. Stephen sighs and jumps in after him.
  Cut to: Cabin. John, as a hugely double-taking old man is staring and gulping and starting in the background.

Hugh Who? What? I . . . what the? I . . . who? But . . . I never . . . oh
God . . . what the . . . how many?
Stephen There now, there now. Take it easy.
Hugh But I . . . I should be dead. How the hell did I . . .? Who are you?
Stephen Me? Clarence Cosy, angel, second class. And your name is Rupert.
Hugh How did you know that?

John's goggling takes and double-takes propel him backwards. He looks at his tea-pot and shakes his head.

Stephen I've granted your wish. You've never been born.
Hugh Oh Jesus. That's all I need. Hey!

He rubs his chin and is amazed to discover that he is no longer unshaven and he no longer has a cut coming from his lip.

  Well shag me twice.
Stephen What's that?
Hugh Water must have healed my cut.
Stephen What cut? There's never been any cut. You were never born.
Hugh Look, angel, do us a favour, will you? Fly away, for Chrissakes.
Stephen Can't. Haven't got my wings yet.
John *(goggling)* Doh!
Hugh I'm getting out of here.

Hugh runs out into the street. Hugh looks with amazement at an empty parking space.

Stephen	Oh great. That's all I need. Now some cockwit has stolen my sodding car. *(coming up behind)* But you haven't got a car. You were never born, Rupert.
Hugh	Look, I don't know who you are, and I don't know under what law you have been released into the community, but just frig off will you?
Stephen	Angels don't frig, Rupert. We don't have the training.
Hugh	Look. Get this, tiny Tim. I own the largest conglomeration of newspaper and satellite television companies in the world, and right now I have better things to do than stand here talking to a chocolate cake like you.
Stephen	Oh dear. Don't you understand? I am your guardian angel. I'm going to show you what this town would have been like if you hadn't been born. That way I'll show you that your life *is* worth living after all. The countless differences you've made to people's lives, the joy you've spread, the difference you've made.
Hugh	I'm going home. Where's a bloody mini-cab?

A black London taxi pulls up and John, the cheery driver, pulls down the window.

John	Where to, guv?
Hugh	Wapping High Street ... wait a minute ...
Stephen	See? What a difference you made?

Inside the cab.

If you'd never been born, there would still be black cabs like this, with drivers who actually know where they're going. But you came along and told everyone that black cabs were a wicked monopoly, and that everyone had better use mini cabs belonging to the company that you own. Knackered old Datsuns with no brakes and drivers who've just escaped from Pentonville.

Hugh	I did that?
Stephen	Exactly. You see? You made a difference.

The cab pulls up and Stephen and Hugh get out. Stephen pays off the driver, who departs with a cheery wave. Hugh looks round the street.

Hugh	Wait an arsing second here. Where the hell are all the satellite dishes?
Stephen	There aren't any.

Hugh	What the...?
Stephen	You haven't been born, I keep telling you. People don't have satellite television, they don't have the chance to watch *World Wrestling* and *Wheel of Fortune* and *Video Bloopers* twenty-four hours a day. They're still forced to sit and watch BBC and ITV, with all those drama and sport and news programmes. You did away with all that.
Hugh	I did?
Stephen	Swept it away. You pretended it was to give people more choice, but it was actually just to make you fabulously rich.
Hugh	Wow.
Stephen	Come on.

Inside a pub. Black and white patrons, standing shoulder to shoulder.

Hugh	Steady on. Not my kind of place.
Stephen	What do you mean?
Hugh	Black people.
Stephen	Don't you like black people?
Hugh	Well, I mean, I don't think they're gonna like me much...
Stephen	No, no, no. I keep telling you. Because you've never been born, the *Sun* newspaper has never been able to tell anyone to hate their neighbour because they're black, or gay, or left-wing. Without you, people have grown up liking each other. And liking this country. They might even like you.

Hugh is leafing through a tabloid paper, while Stephen orders a couple of drinks.

Hugh	Jesus mothering arse! Where the hell are the tits?
Stephen	They're on the front of women's chests. I think the editor probably thought it wasn't much of a news story.
Hugh	Yeah, but you've got to have tits to sell a paper...

The barman brings the drinks.

Stephen	Well apparently not. Apparently, without the *Sun* debasing people's view of the world with every sentence it produces, people turn out to be interested in all sorts of other things. Strange, isn't it?

The drinks arrive and Hugh pushes aside Stephen's offer to pay.

Hugh	I'll get these.

He brings out some coins and stops.

Bloody hell. Who's this?

He holds up a coin showing the Queen's head.

Stephen   It's the Queen. They still have one, you see.

People start singing a carol in the background.

Hugh   Christ, get me the cock out of here.

Stephen and Hugh walk through the street back towards the bridge.

(looking over the bridge) It's brilliant. Totally bloody brilliant. Big red buses, free hospitals, an amusing royal family, proper taxis, decent newspapers, best television in the world. People getting on with each other . . .

Stephen   You like it? You really like it?

Hugh   It's fantastic. It's paradise. Help me Clarence, please, I want to live again. Jeez.

Stephen   Well, Rupert, this is marvellous news I must say.

Hugh   Just think of the money I could make in a world like this. I could introduce big tits, I could break up the broadcasting monopolies, I could destroy *The Times*, the BBC, the Royal Family, I could make a bloody fortu —

Stephen pushes him over the side and watches him fall.

Stephen   Twat.

VOX POP   **Hugh** My wife was pulled down the other day and rebuilt just north of Leicester. Damn shame.

Dog Hamper

Hugh is striding about in the middle of a disgusting mall. He is rather pukka and excitedly leading the camera hither and thither.

Hugh   It's extraordinary. I should say the house was exactly here. The front door must have been there, round about where that branch of Next is. Of course all around this area was our garden. When my dog Hamper died, border collie with the loveliest laugh, it was the saddest day of my life. Couldn't believe Hamper was really dead, but my father insisted he was. Harsh lesson. Learnt young. Anyway, part of the process of grieving is burial, so I buried him, I should think round about here, under this paving stone it must have been.

Hugh kicks the paving stone and it comes loose.

Whoops . . . so much for 1990s build quality, eh?

The whole slab comes off and a border collie climbs out.

Good Lord, Hamper! I was right all along. Come along then, you'll be hungry.

VOX POP **Stephen** *(female)* You can't even trust professionals these days. I went to see a masseur, you know for a massage. Disgusting. He couldn't keep his hands off me.

Child Abuse

A fuzzy, amateurish-looking video shot of Stephen and Hugh in some kind of office. Record of an official interview. Hugh speaks softly and caringly.

Hugh	Where did he touch you, can you remember?
Stephen	Er ... on the hand, I suppose.
Hugh	On the hand, I see. Which hand, do you remember?
Stephen	Er ... right, usually.
Hugh	Right usually, I see. Was it violent?
Stephen	Well ... firm.
Hugh	Firm. Firm. Alright. Now, I've got a doll here. Can you show me with the doll exactly what he used to do?

Hugh brings out an Action Man and hands it to Stephen.

Stephen	He didn't use a doll.
Hugh	No, no. Pretend the doll is you, and show me what he used to do.
Stephen	Right, well ... he would take my hand like this, and he would move it up and down a few times like this.

Stephen shakes hands with the Action Man.

Hugh	And this happened every day, you say?
Stephen	Every day, when he left for work. Except weekends. He stayed at home at weekends, so there was no need for him to shake my hand, I suppose.
Hugh	Right. And did he threaten you? Make you promise to keep this little secret of yours?
Stephen	No.
Hugh	You don't remember.
Stephen	No, I do remember. He didn't threaten me.
Hugh	Well, let's say that you don't remember not remembering.
Stephen	No, I do remember remembering, because I remember thinking – I must remember this.
Hugh	You're in denial.
Stephen	I'm sorry.
Hugh	Denial, is what we call the state that you are currently in.
Stephen	Denial, as everyone knows, is in Egypt.

Young Tory of the Year

Stephen, in drag, is in a box at a concert hall, a packed house behind him and an orchestra tuning up.

Stephen   Hello and three dozen welcomes to the *Harrogate Young Tory of the Year*, here at the Daily Mail Hall, Horrorgate, in front of an invited audience of local businessmen and their slightly awkward teenage children in pony-tails and annoying ties. With me is one of the judges, Brent Wheeler, and he'll be giving expert advice and telling us what to look out for. Good evening Brent.

Hugh   Quite right.

Stephen   Brent, the standard last year was incredibly high, do you think we can look for something similar this year?

Hugh   Well, Susan, I think we probably can. I've been a judge for some of the local heats and I can tell you the talent this year is as awesome as ever it's been.

Stephen   This being the night of the finals, the competitors will be concentrating on keynote speeches and displays of general prejudice and ignorance, is that right?

Hugh   More or less. There is a new round this year, however, a Getting Shiny-faced in a T-shirt round.

Stephen   T-shirt? That sounds very . . .

Hugh   Well, this is the way modern Young Toryism is being developed. T-shirts show that it isn't just an art for the middle classes, but has general American street fashion-wise appeal for the young and hip-trendy.

Stephen   Right, well. The lights are going down behind me as you can probably hear, and our first competitor, Andrew Tredgold is ready to go on.

Hugh, as a Young Tory, Andrew Tredgold, steps on to the stage with a speech. There is a blue cyclorama behind with a Union Jack-Arrow logo and the slogan 'Forward with into Britain tomorrow right step'.

(*hushed voice*) Andrew is in his second year at Exeter reading Human Bigotry and Libertarian Nonsense. He counts amongst his inspirations the 'Family Values' theme by Kevin Patten, the 'Further Cuts in Public Expenditure' suite by Kenneth Clarke, arranged Portillo, and the 'Endless Variations in J. Major'. So, Andrew Tredgold, South West regional winner.

Hugh stands in front of those perspex autocue screens and clears his throat. Stephen is the conductor, à la Simon Rattle. The orchestra plays 'I Vow to Thee my Country' underneath. Andrew watches nervously as Stephen gives him a reassuring smile and then cues him.

Hugh	(*as Andrew: becoming* incredibly *fast*) Conference. Core values, real punishment for offenders, family standards, opportunity for individual enterprise, roll back the frontiers of the state, Michael's bold and imaginative initiative, and yes, why not corporal punishment, really crack down, young offenders, rule of law, and yes I make no apology, respect for ordinary decent vast majority, welfare spongers, as Norman said so clearly, individual enterprise culture, opportunity attack on trendy liberal educational wishy-washy to pick up on Kevin's wonderfully forceful point, sloppy thinking, sixties, in Michael's bold and imaginative values, standards, decency, family, law, yes, I make no apology and why not even perhaps, God and pride in country, decent ordinary sloppy people, vast majority of bold new initiatives, decent, family standards, core values, return to fifties, responsibility, individual, respect, standard, values, and yes, why not, values, respect, standards, ordinary, decent apology, I make no standards, vast family law, and why not sloppy corporal God punishment individual decent spongers wishy-washy trendy family crime Michael values. Thank you.

Huge applause.

Stephen	Well, the audience absolutely loving Andrew's performance there. But what will the judges make of it, I wonder? Brent.
Hugh	Well, it was wonderfully confident and assured, wasn't it? Original, though. I'm not sure how much the judges will like that. Did you notice in one of the earlier passages he opted for 'family standards' instead of the more classically correct 'family values'? But the technique was astonishing for one his age: he was every bit as insulting as a Tory twice his age.
Stephen	Any actual mistakes?
Hugh	Not real mistakes, no.
Stephen	I thought at one point that he was going to say something that made sense.
Hugh	He *just* managed to avoid that, didn't he? A tense moment. But, no. Very assured, very ghastly: completely sucked dry of youth, energy, ideals, imagination, love, passion or intelligence.
Stephen	Well, while the audience vomit we'll return you to the shop where we bought you.

Interrogation

Stephen, as a solicitor, sits at a table in a police interview room, next to Kevin, his client. Hugh sits opposite with Fiona, a WPC, next to him. Kevin is upset.

Kevin   Yes, yes I admi...

Hugh holds up a hand to silence Kevin.

Hugh   *(switching on recorder: speaking in routine monotone)*Wednesday 4th April 1994, 18.32 hours. Detective Sergeant Carter interviewing Jonathan Dumayne, Mr William Ponce, solicitor and WPC...

Stephen   And commissioner for oaths...

Hugh   And commissioner for oaths, and WPC Helen Thompson are also in attendance. Mr Parker has been advised of his rights.

Hugh appears to have finished.

Kevin   I...

Hugh   This interview is being conducted in accordance with the Police and Criminal Evidence Act 1987, Section 17, Interview Procedure, and is being recorded on chromium dioxide tape, with Dolby C noise reduction engaged, delivering magnetic tape registration through twin direct drive spindle-heads tracking at 57 revolutions per minute outputting 200 watts per channel. The unit is powered by alternating current at 240 volts with a maximum of 7.5 amps.

Again Hugh seems to have shot his bolt.

Kevin   I don't really know why I...

Hugh   Mr Parker is wearing a light grey worsted wool jacket with slashed pockets and double vent with a configuration of three buttons, at present unfastened. His shirt is a woollen cotton mix of the type commonly known as Vyella. No tie. His trousers...

Hugh looks under the table.

...are a dark blue drill cotton, in the diagonal weave often referred to as chino. Odd socks and a pair of Air Wear shoes, known as DMs, short for Doctor Marten, the inventor of this brand of cushioned rubber sole which is acid splash resistant, hardy, comfortable and pleasantly styled. The prisoner is currently refreshing himself with a cup of tea and a biscuit brought by the duty sergeant. He has chosen an English breakfast blend taken with semi-skimmed milk and a half teaspoonful of the low calorie aspartame sweetener Candarel Spoonful which can help reduce weight only as part of a calorie-controlled diet. Of the range of quality biscuits on offer he selected a McVitie's Boaster. The prisoner is aware that this interview is being recorded.

Hugh has apparently shot his bolt. Kevin is doubtful. He opens his mouth, finds that Hugh isn't going to speak, so starts himself.

Kevin	I suppose I just . . .
Hugh	Mr Ponce has opted for a suit of slate grey herring-bone, from the Marks & Spencer Elegance range, teamed with a two-fold poplin shirt . . . collar stiffeners?

Stephen nods.

	Mr Ponce has indicated that collar stiffeners are inserted.
Stephen	In the collars.
Hugh	WPC Thompson is wearing regulation Metropolitan Police white blouse . . .
Fiona	Blouson.
Hugh	I beg your pardon, blouson with . . . what colour would you call that skirt?
Fiona	Navy.
Hugh	. . . navy skirt with chequered tie-thing.
Fiona	Stock.
Hugh	. . . with chequered stock. I note the application of a coral lipstick and an amber foundation cream of the colouring known as Gay Whisper.

Fiona nods that this is correct.

	Her hair is attractively arranged with a delightful cow-lick reminiscent of the 1960s model Jean Shrimpton and the styling techniques of the then fashionable Vidal Sassoon. A light day-time fragrance has been applied to her pulse-points. The citrus top-notes with a deep bass of vetiver and wood-bark tells me that the favoured scent is Diorella, by Christian Dior of Paris, New York and London.
Fiona	Dioressence.
Hugh	Damn.
Fiona	Very close . . .
Hugh	Dioressence, by Christian Dior of the previously mentioned cities. Right, Mr Dumayne . . .

Hugh has stopped. After a couple of false starts Kevin realises his moment has come.

Kevin   I am extremely happy to tell you the full facts of the...

There is a loud clunk. They all look at the machine. Then at the camera. A trumpet goes: MWA MWA MWA...

VOX POP **Hugh** As I travel round the country, giving speeches and replacing lengths of guttering in high buildings, I have become increasingly distressed at the ignorance and prejudice that seems to surround the whole business of sucking. This used to be a dynamic nation; a nation of skill and know-how, of determination and vision. The rest of the world used to look to us for a lead on sucking, and we were happy, proud I should say, to give it. Now, well you can ask the average Briton to suck something for you in the street, even something quite small, like a hedge, and like as not he'll just shrug his shoulders and move on. That's sad. Terribly, terribly sad.

Avenger

Fiona grins nervously at the camera.

Fiona   Hello.

Pause.

Doesn't seem to be anybody here. I expect one of them'll turn up in a minute.

Pause.

But for the time being, it rather looks as if I'm sort of ... on my own ...

Stephen's voice booms out from nowhere, lots of echo.

Stephen   That's right, my dear. You are quite, quite alone.
Fiona   Who's that?

Fiona looks round the studio. The camera zooms into odd things like lamps and coffee cups. Lily Marlene starts playing, cracklingly.

Stephen   The fog has settled on the moor, and may not lift for days.
Fiona   Show yourself. Who are you?
Stephen   Come, my dear, don't say that you've forgotten?
Fiona   Forgotten who? What...?
Stephen   Welwyn Garden City. 1974. Debenhams car park.
Fiona   Max?
Stephen   I waited, Fiona. I waited a long, long time. But you never came. Why didn't you come, Fiona? I waited ...
Fiona   The traffic ... I had a flat headache ... my wife turned up ... the fire burnt down ... oh what's the use ... oh Max, Max, Max ...

Fiona collapses on to the sofa, sobbing. When she looks up, Stephen is standing over her.

Stephen   I have waited a long time for this moment.
Fiona   Max, I'm sorry.
Stephen   Sorry? Sorry? You think you can leave me with three bags of quite heavy shopping, run off to Paris with your lover-dancing-boy-laugher, and then say 'sorry'?
Fiona   Max, you don't understand ... I was young, I was in love ...

Hugh comes on.

Hugh   Hello. Fiona? M'colleague. What's going on?

Fiona and Stephen assume airs of complete innocence.

Stephen   Nothing.
Fiona   Nothing at all.
Stephen   We were just chatting.
Hugh   Fiona. You look fabulous like that. Alive. Feline. Arousing.
Stephen   No ... *(pointing to Fiona)* ... that's Fiona.
Hugh   Oh.

VOX POP Hugh Big ones, small ones, thin ones, fat ones, stiff ones, floppy ones, ones that hang to the left, ones that hang to the right. I'm talking of course, about penises. What are they for? They expel waste fluids from the male bladder, they serve as a conduit in the process of insemination, but what else? You can't live in them. You can't drive them. You can't wear them. You can't borrow money from them at any rates, never mind favourable ones, so all in all, what good are they? I wrote to the Duchess of Kent to find out. I haven't received an answer yet.

Going for Gold

Hugh is Henry Kelly. Stephen is Colin. Beside him are Kevin and Fiona and Andrea.

Hugh Hello and welcome to *English People Appear to be the Most Ignorant in Europe.* I shall be asking questions of our three likely contestants, Dieter Schomer, who is a dental technician from Hamburg, Andrea Larsen, who is a dental technician from Oslo, and Colin Mint, who is a dental technician from Tunbridge Wells in Kent. Let's go straight into the first round. Dieter, your question. I am a female journalist who came to fame in the 1960s, presenting *Blue Peter...*

Kevin Valerie Singleton.

Hugh Correct. Andrea. I am an underground station on London's Northern Line, situated between Warren Street and Tottenham Court...

Andrea Goodge Street...

Hugh Correct. Colin. Ich bin ein geflunsigge sturmfische, betolden lemhausen feuneubische, stem hamburg von ledentrader masch fenvarsentleiter und grobbische.

Stephen looks vacant.

Have a guess...

Stephen Mary Queen of Scots.

Hugh The answer I was looking for, Colin, was William Waldegrave. Bad luck. *(To camera.)* Ladies and gentlemen, we're thrilled to be able to present this next item. Dame Victoria Bennett stars in Alan Wood's acclaimed prestige dramatic monologue *Well I Never Did.*

Gossiping Heads

Beautifully shot in video, like the Talking Heads *programmes, we see a northern front room. Stephen is sitting there, in drag, a cup of tea and a biscuit in one hand, a family album in the other. He looks through some photographs.*

Stephen   Oh, yes ... yes ... well, I'll never forget this one. That was before they pulled down the gasworks and built that Netto Superstore. Oh, he looks good in his Littlewood's Keynote cardie, does our Alan. I said at the time, I said 'Alan, if you want to get on in the world, you'd be wise to write down everything I say, because it's gold, is what I say. And don't hog the Peak Freenes, lad. Pass them round.' Lovely boy he was. Teeth weren't his strong feature, of course, and his hair wasn't what you'd call Leslie Howard, but I always say, 'Teeth is teeth, what does it matter so long as you've got your wealth?' He said, 'I can't wait to get out of here, Auntie Ivy, and make my fortune down south.' I said to him, straight, I said, 'Alan,' I said, 'I may not be as cabbage looking as my tongue is a fisherman's doiley, but what's London got that you won't find in the Arndale Centre in Todmodern?' Well, he was stuck for a reply. I said, 'You want sophistication, you stick with us up here, love.' He knew I was right, bless him. I mean we've got a Body Shop in the parade now and you can't move for Volvo's in the autumn months. But then he's always had his head in the clouds has our Alan. Caught him trying to scour a milk pan with a tea bag once. I said 'It's all very well knowing long words, but if you can't tell the difference between a box of brillo pad and a packet of Typhoo One-Cup, you'll never get on.' I'll go to the back of our fridge.

He did leave, though. Got a scholarship to Oxford. I said, 'You make sure as there's somewhere as you can buy Kendall Mint Cake, and a good bar of Wright's coal tar soap, because they've no idea, down there.' Well, I mean fancy ideas and tropical mix croutons are all very well, but they don't get the Vimto buttered, do they? For all your fine Italian red lettuce, which to my mind tastes as bitter as a Skipton wind. He said 'Auntie Ivy, I'll be fine.' Well of course I didn't know him when he came back. Green corduroy jacket and duffle coat, horn-rimmed spectacles you could eat parsley out of and a head crammed with I don't know what. And books, you've never seen so many. Some of them that dirty I blushed to the roots of my Playtex. I said, 'Alan,' I said, 'those books are going straight into the Hotpoint and no buts.' Came up lovely they did. Amazing what a bit of Lenor can do if you've a mind. No, but that Oxford and his smart friends, they've changed him. Ideas, that's what it is. I said, 'What use is ideas when you've a capon to baste and the tally-man's due any minute? Name an idea,' I said, 'that can get the front steps scrubbed, the sausages pricked and the navel oranges squeezed in time for a meat tea and finger buffet.' Well, he didn't know which way to look. These Oxford types, they're all apricot facial scrub and yesterday's suet turnover: to look at them you'd think a packet of Bachelor's Savoury Rice wouldn't melt in their Vosene Medicated, but they've no savvy. I could take a Black and Decker nose drill to the pack of them and still have change left over for a bag of peanut brittle.

Left home of course, got involved with the BBC, all party eggs and tomato chutney. Next thing I know he's got a damehood and a brand new hostess trolley to show for it. They'll fall for anything them Londoners. Well, I'm off down to Morrison's for a jar of melon lip balm and a four-pack of interuterine devices. Got that Pat Routledge round for elocution lessons at twelve. Tarra.

VOX POP **Hugh** Okay, so the woman was mad. She was mad, she was paranoid, she was megalomaniac and she was completely deluded. But somehow when she was in charge, you know, Blue Peter was Blue Peter.

Fascion

Hugh sits on the edge of a desk and talks to camera, in front of a portrait of Adolf Hitler, and assorted swastika-like symbols.

Hugh	You know, there's been a lot in the news recently, about the rise of fascism. It's the next big thing, they say, but what exactly is it? What kind of music do fascists listen to? What do they wear? Are there clubs you can go to? Kevin, you're an old fascist from way back, what's it all about?
Kevin	Well, what first got me hooked was the uniform ...
Hugh	Do you have your uniform with you at all?
Kevin	Well, I'm wearing it now.
Hugh	Oh that's it, is it?
Kevin	Yeah. It's very comfortable, hard-wearing, and I just ... I don't know ... I think I look good in it.
Hugh	You do, Kevin, you look marvellous. If I was homosexual, I'd want to buy you a drink at the very least.
Kevin	Thanks. If I was homosexual, I'd have a pint of lager.
Hugh	As it is, I like birds.
Kevin	Me too.
Hugh	Now Kevin. Music. What sort of music do you listen to? What's your thing? What's your bag? What's your ... I suppose what I'm trying to say is, what sort of music do you listen to?
Kevin	Oh all sorts. Military bands, bit of Wagner ...
Hugh	Because Hitler liked a bit of all that, didn't he?
Kevin	He certainly did ...
Hugh	Now, for the people watching, it's worth pointing out that Hitler was quite a big name in the fascism business ... what, back in the seventies ...
Kevin	Even earlier than that ...
Hugh	Earlier than the seventies, wow. Right in there at the beginning. Like a sort of Elvis figure.
Kevin	Yeah ...
Hugh	Now tell me about Hitler. There's been a lot of stuff written about him, magazine profiles and all that ... what do you think he was really like?
Kevin	He was a wild guy.
Hugh	That's what I'd heard. I'd heard he liked to live on the edge ...
Kevin	Absolutely.
Hugh	Wow, that's really interesting. Did he have a philosophy, at all? I mean, was he a Kevin Lennon kind of guy?

Kevin	The supremacy of the Aryan race was his sort of inspiration, I suppose.
Hugh	Yeah, and a sort of segregationy thing, I suppose?
Kevin	Yeah. Racial purity...
Hugh	Racial purity, all that stuff... But of course, tragically, he died, didn't he?
Kevin	That's right.
Hugh	Drugs, was it? I think...
Kevin	He shot himself...
Hugh	Oh that's really sad. I guess he must have been depressed, or something.

VOX POP Stephen (*as woman: holds up a Body-Form Ultra*) It's ever so thin. Much thinner than conventional towels. That's an advantage. The disadvantage is that you need about twelve just to dry your hair. Conventional towels have the edge there, I feel.

Operational Criteria

Kevin is in a patient's bed in a hospital room. Fiona, his devoted wife, sits at his side. Stephen is examining him, be-white-coated. He has a stethoscope to Kevin's chest.

Hugh suddenly enters, dressed as a nurse, and speaks with unaccustomed ferocity to the camera.

Hugh	Yes, alright, it's a sketch in a hospital ward. I'm so sorry. I'm so sorry that we're not breaking moulds and deconstructing forms and pushing envelopes and drinking strange new types of lager in underground bars with tight hipster jeans hanging from our earlobes. I'm sorry we haven't 'raised interesting questions' about the nature of gender assignment, or peeled back the veneer of cultural denial. I am so nose-blowingly sorry.
Stephen	You're not at all.
Hugh	You're damn bloody right I'm not. It's a hospital room, he's a doctor, he's a patient. Oh dear. Oh arsing dear, what a disappointment. Where are the challenged perceptions there, I don't wonder for a single hair-gelled bloody minute?

Hugh goes.

Stephen	Say 'ah'.
Kevin	Ah.
Stephen	Say 'twim'.
Kevin	Twim.
Stephen	Twim.
Kevin	Twim.
Stephen	Fadabberhaweeeeee.
Kevin	Fadabberhaweeeeee.
Stephen	Twim.
Kevin	Twim.

Hugh comes back in, really angry.

Hugh	They do still exist, you know. Hospitals. Just because a lot of twats in leather waistcoats and black polo-necks fart their way through the *Late Show* talking about 'tapping into the dark underbelly of British social repression', doesn't mean that hospitals don't exist, or that people don't go to them when they're ill.
Stephen	Hugh?
Hugh	What?
Stephen	Get out.

Hugh goes.

Fiona	Well, Doctor?
Stephen	Well, Doctor, yes. Hmm. Alright, situation is this. We have a heart, standing by, ready to go. Nice little heart, too. Red, which is the only colour, really, for hearts, I always think. Pump pump pump. That side of things is all fine.
Fiona	Oh thank God . . .
Stephen	But, and this is a pretty fat but, you . . . are a smoker, are you not, Mr Spiers?
Kevin	I occasionally . . .
Stephen	You occasionally smoke cigarettes, yes, I thought so.
Fiona	Is that a problem?
Stephen	It is, rather, I'm afraid. Puts us in a hell of a position. Mr Twovey doesn't smoke, you see.
Kevin	Who's Mr Twovey?
Stephen	Nice chap, two rooms down. Came in just after you, also hoping for a heart. Never smoked in his life. Or smoked once, rather, but didn't inhale. So he says.
Fiona	You mean . . . you're going to give it to him? The one heart you've got, you're going to give to Mr Twovey?
Stephen	Not necessarily. As I say, he's a nice enough chap, but by God, you should see him eating soup.
Kevin	Soup?
Stephen	Revolting sight. Slurping and sucking, spilling it all over the place . . . quite revolting.
Kevin	Yes?
Stephen	Now I've watched you eating soup, Mr Spiers, and it's rather an attractive sight. You hold the spoon properly, tilt the bowl away from you, suck out of the side of the spoon rather than the end, and you're very neat about it. Very neat indeed.
Fiona	So . . .
Stephen	So, you're more or less level on that score. You don't dress as well as he does . . .
Kevin	Don't I?

Stephen opens the cupboard next to the bed.

Stephen	Look at this. Ghastly Viyella check shirt, simply doesn't go with this jacket . . . whereas Mr Twovey came in in a very elegant two-button dark grey flannel suit.
Fiona	I told you to wear the blue shirt. I said, wear the blue shirt . . .
Stephen	But at least you don't bite your finger nails, that's something.

Kevin	No, that's right. I don't. Or I may have done once, but I didn't inhale . . .
Stephen	Twovey's a real chewer. Revolting, stumpy little fingernails. Makes me sick to look at them. No, this really is a tricky one . . .

Stephen deliberates. Kevin and Fiona look at each other in desperation.

Fiona	He does a lot of work in the community . . .
Stephen	I'm sorry?
Fiona	Gerald is very active within the community . . .
Stephen	Hmm. I've never quite understood what that means . . . I mean, burglars are very active within the community . . .
Fiona	But Gerald does a lot of good work . . . and his family are very fond of him . . .
Stephen	Mr Twovey's family are devoted to him . . .
Fiona	Does ever such a lot for *Children In Need* and *Comic Relief*.
Stephen	Mr Twovey once spent the whole day in women's clothes for the ITV *Telethon.*
Fiona	Gerald once met Esther Rantzen.
Stephen	Did you indeed?
Kevin	Yes, but I didn't inhale.
Stephen	Mm. Eeny, meeny, miney . . . yes, Nurse, what is it?

Hugh has entered. He whispers into Stephen's ear. On his way out he flicks a V at the camera.

	Well, there's a relief. We do now have another heart in, so we can service you both.
Kevin	Never!
Fiona	Oh, Doctor that's . . . can I kiss you?
Stephen	If I can punch you violently in the throat, yes. Now. Since I'm here I might as well give you first choice. The first heart comes from a young squash player, twenty-five, from Aberdeen, and this new one's from a sixty-five-year-old Tory Cabinet Minister.
Kevin	Oh I'll take the Cabinet Minister's, definitely.
Stephen	Why?
Kevin	Because it's never been used.

Stephen, Kevin and Fiona all turn to the camera and smile winningly. Hugh comes on and glares.

Fan Club

Stephen and Hugh address the nation.

Hugh You know, we've had a whole armpitful of letters from a viewer recently, asking whether she can join the Fry & Laurie Fan Club, and I'm afraid, Giselle of Nuneaton, the answer is no, because there isn't one.

Stephen Wasn't one.

Hugh That's right. There also wasn't one, as well as there being an isn't one.

Stephen What a magical weaver of words you are, Hugh.

Hugh Cheers.

Stephen What I mean is, there wasn't one, but there is one now.

Hugh Hello?

Stephen Or rather there are two.

Hugh We've got one each? Shrewd. Very shrewd.

Stephen No, our legs have got one each.

Hugh Sorry?

Stephen One club is called the Fry & Laurie Left Leg Club, and the other is called . . .

Hugh Don't tell me . . . no, actually you'd better tell me.

Stephen The Fry & Laurie Right Leg Club. For the frighteningly reasonable sum of £450 a month, you will be entitled to a yearly newsletter, containing articles, profiles, photographs, competitions, crosswords, and in-depth interviews with our right legs.

Hugh What extraordinarily good value this offer seems to represent. And does membership of the Right Leg Club give you automatic membership of the Left Leg Club?

Stephen Sadly no, Hugh. We may be generous, but we're not nice.

Hugh Gotcha.

Stephen Membership of the Left Leg Club however is slightly cheaper, at £390 a month.

Hugh Now why would that be, I wonder?

Stephen I don't know. Marketing boys came up with it.

Hugh Interesting. Couldn't we get any grown-ups to do our marketing?

Stephen But if you join both clubs at once, you will be entitled to this T-shirt . . .

Stephen holds up a plain white T-shirt.

. . . with our famous catchphrase on it. We will also send you a fully automatic Frank Windsor as part of this once-in-a-lifetime introductory offer.

Picture of Frank Windsor flashes up on the screen.

Anyway, that's enough merchandising news. Until the same time next week, eat plenty of hot meals and take heaps of exercise.

Hugh   Oh and . . .

Stephen Shut up.

VOX POP **Stephen** I get this terrible reaction, when I eat chocolate. I get awful rashes all over my body, and this odd, greeny-blue pus starts to leak out from my armpits, revolting smell, and I get these terrible pains up and down my legs, I sometimes just scream for hours with the agony of it, and then my liver fails altogether and I usually have to be rushed into casualty and have a drip put in my arm, and all the time I've got these headaches that make me think my brain is going to explode, and I'm covered in pus, my liver gone, legs burning pain and I say to myself, I couldn't half murder a Twix.

The Duke of Northampton

Aerial shot of a large stately home. Grand music.

  Stephen is standing in his study, stroking a labrador. Hugh, in a dress, is sitting on a sofa, petting a spaniel.

Stephen	I suppose in a way we are very lucky. A lot of people would consider us very privileged. Actually, you see, I don't own Hartington Castle. It doesn't actually belong to me.
Voice off	Yes it does.
Stephen	Yes. It does. It *does*. In that sense it does. I do own it. But I think, I always think, that actually I've simply borrowed it.
Voice	Who from?
Stephen	From my children.
Hugh	*(softly)* That's lovely.
Stephen	It's a trust. I'm just the bloody caretaker, you know? Just the bloody old caretaker.
Hugh	We don't really use this room, do we?
Stephen	That's right. My grandfather used this room. They say Lloyd George vomited in that awful old silver bucket thing over there.
Hugh	We rather hate that, don't we?
Stephen	Can't stand the sight of it. Now this is rather fun ...

Stephen takes a small metal object from a display case.

Hugh	Great fun ...
Stephen	Have a guess at what that might be.

Close-up of the object.

Voice	Oyster knife?

Stephen chuckles richly. So does Hugh.

Stephen	A lot of people say that. Actually it's not an oyster knife. Have another guess.

Interviewer says something we can't quite hear.

Not that. I don't even know what an interuterine device is, actually. Have another guess. *(Pause.)* No? I'll tell you. It's just a knife. An ordinary knife. We keep it here. Can't sell the bloody thing of course. Costs a fortune just to keep it heated. But it's rather fun and it's a heck of a thought that my great grandchildren will take it out some time next century.

Hugh	Such fun.
Stephen	(*putting it back carefully*) Great fun.

Cut to garden. Hugh is pruning roses in the background and doing something rather silly with them. Stephen stands by a fountain.

That's the challenge of course. You know. One's descendants. If my bloody ancestors ... mostly a gang of old crooks actually ... if *they* could keep this damned thing going, without the advantage of mains shopping and what have you, then ... you know, as I say. This (*pointing at flower bed*) is rather interesting, actually. The third Duke, I think it was, had these beds planted out, very much the thing then, of course.

Hugh falls over in the background.

And apparently the soil that existed in the beds was completely wrong, so what do you think he did? They thought big in those days, of course. Well, he had over four hundredweight of the right soil transported from all the way over there.

Points to a place about three yards away.

Got assorted locals to help ... whole village turned out ... stood them all cider and badger cakes afterwards, that sort of thing. But I tell you ... that sort of *vision*, you know? If I tried to do that sort of thing now they'd say I was crackers, have me locked up and sewing potatoes soon as look at me, I expect.

Cut to Hugh in another part of the garden. There is a gardener.

Hugh	(*to interviewer*) The summer can be pretty ghastly. Open days and lots of coaches filing in and gawping and peering and so on with their muddy tyres everywhere. (*To gardener.*) I don't like the look of those aphids at all, Godfrey.
Gardener	I could spray them tomorrow, your Grace.
Hugh	(*tartly*) No, thank you. I shan't want them sprayed tomorrow, I don't think. I've never been much of a one for having things sprayed tomorrow. (*Back to interviewer.*) Actually people can be rather fun. I remember one enormous lady in pink who was staring at this rather ugly and impossible lacquered cabinet in the Chinese room and she turned to her husband, who was a very funny little man in tight trousers, you know the sort of

thing, and she said, ''Ere, Bert ... we could do with one of them in our front lounge parlour.' Rather priceless. Great fun.

The gardener has been considering.

Gardener   I could spray them this afternoon.
Hugh   I don't think so. I rather hate things being sprayed in the afternoon. *(Walking away.)* No. Not that, thank you.

Stephen is in his study.

Stephen   A certain amount of pressure is brought to bear, obviously, in the matter of children. Got to provide an heir to take over this lot when I'm dead and gone and buried and no longer alive. Mary does most of the work there. It's something of a tradition in our family that the wife actually carries the child in her stomach before it's born. I let her look after all that side of things. Absolutely wonderful at it too. Can't stand most of the children, great ugly things, take up a huge amount of room and the devil to keep them heated and free of damp. But you know, that's all part of the job.

Cut to wonderful dining-room. Hugh is sitting reading the **Telegraph.** *Four hundred dogs are scampering about. A servant is pouring coffee. Over this Stephen comes down.*

I call it the 'job', you know. Most people probably imagine being a Duke is just one long round of parties and fête openings and so on. To me it's a job, like any other. Like everyone else, I have to get up at ten, I have to put my own clothes on as they've been laid out ... I come down to breakfast, just like any person would. And then I might talk to the estate manager about the farms, discuss the state of the coverts with my gamekeepers and Mary and I will run over the events of the day ... who's coming to dinner, what menus we should arrange with the kitchens. It's really no different from being a coal-welder or floor walker at your local Asda.

Sound of Hugh and Stephen discussing the day.

Hugh   And we absolutely must decide on the May Day Claimings.

Hugh and Stephen begin to discuss names of villagers. They talk about Martha, young Lucy, Tabetha and so on.

Stephen   *(over)* One rather charming local custom around here in the local

41

	neighbourhood that surrounds the immediate environs of the nearby area locally is the May Day Claimings, so called. Mary and I feel a great responsibility to keep up with those things. Otherwise one can lose touch.
Hugh	*(over)* When I married Charles he warned me that what he calls his 'job' does entail a lot of public responsibility and duty and I'm very keen to share that where possible.
Stephen	The point of the Claimings is that I have to choose a young girl to lead the May Day procession in the village. She must be no older than sixteen and no younger than fourteen. She is queen of the May for the day and I have to crown her and, after the maypole dancing and all that sort of palaver, I take her to the dungeons in the old part of the castle and privately violate her.
Hugh	We always have great fun choosing the girls. It's one of those very silly English customs whose point is lost in the mists of which there are plenty round here. But it would be such a pity to lose the connection with history.
Stephen	It derives, I *think*, from some time in the seventies when my father thought that violating a village maiden would be rather a good idea. I think that's the origin, though some people claim it goes back as far as 1968. Great fun, though. I always throw myself completely into the spirit of the thing and enjoy it thoroughly.

VOX POP **Hugh** I found this absolutely hilarious misprint in last week's edition of the *Peterborough Echo*. It says . . . listen to this: 'The Prime Minister, Mr John Major is a dignified and impressive leader.' Isn't that priceless?

A.I.

Clive and Imelda are sitting in a waiting-room. Clive is reading a New Yorker. *He looks puzzled, and passes the mag across to Imelda.*

Clive	See that cartoon?
Imelda	Yes?
Clive	What does it mean?

Imelda looks at it for a while.

Imelda	Beats me.

The door opens and Hugh pops his head out.

Hugh	Mr and Mrs Dont?
Clive	That's right.
Hugh	Do come in.

They all move through into Hugh's surgery.

	Now then. *In vitro* fertilisation was your thing, I believe.
Clive	That's right.
Imelda	We found your name pasted up in a phone box on the Finchley Road, and we thought, well, why not?
Hugh	Why not indeed? Free country. You've tried getting pregnant in the normal way, I assume?
Imelda	Well . . .
Clive	Oh yes. We both eat bananas first thing in the morning, and we've drunk out of the same tea-cup more than once, I can tell you.
Hugh	Really?
Clive	Did it in the back of a car, once.
Imelda	(*embarrassed*) Phil . . .
Clive	Well . . . he's a doctor, isn't he?
Hugh	Right. Good. OK, so what would you like?
Imelda	Well, ideally, we'd like a baby.
Clive	Ideally . . .
Hugh	A baby what?
Clive	I'm sorry?
Hugh	Dog, cat, parrot, giraffe, what?
Imelda	Well . . .
Clive	Human, we thought . . .

Hugh	Human, yes, fine, if you like. I've got some brochures here. Basically we can do anything you want. We can take foetuses from surrogate mothers, we can take them from dead mothers, we can take dead foetuses, we can take sperm from just about anywhere, it's up to you. You know. Black babies, white babies, short babies, tall babies. Musical babies, athletic babies, menthol-flavoured babies, you name it . . .
Imelda	Well I think we'd like just . . . a baby, really.
Hugh	Bog standard baby.
Imelda	Please.
Hugh	Right. No distinguishing characteristics at all?
Clive	Well, we would like it to be born in the sign of Gemini.
Hugh	Yeah?
Clive	Yes, that way we reckon he or she is less likely to grow up believing in astrology.
Hugh	Fair enough. And you're sure you want a human baby, are you? Only it's a bit of a growth sector, animals.
Clive	Really?
Hugh	Definitely. Mrs Willis will be having a kangaroo in a couple of months.
Imelda	Good heavens.
Hugh	Seems strange to us, but believe me, to our children it will be the most natural thing in the world. Well, everything seems natural to my children, because they're actually otters. And otters, as you know, take things pretty much in their stride. But you understand my point.
Imelda	We didn't realise there was such a range available.
Clive	It's amazing.
Hugh	Animals make wonderful children, as a matter of fact. What sort of house do you live in? Large? Small?
Clive	Large-ish . . .
Hugh	A bungalow?
Imelda	No.
Hugh	Well, I wouldn't advise your giving birth to badgers then. Badgers hate stairs. How wet is this house of yours?
Clive	Wet?
Hugh	Wet. How wet?
Imelda	Well . . .
Clive	Averagely wet, I'd say.
Hugh	You'd say averagely wet. Averagely wet. I'd probably decide against sea-lions. Wonderful offspring, but they do like a more than averagely wet house. Your best bet is mammal, furry and reasonably friendly. I have a wonderful strain of weasel at the moment.
Clive	Weasel.
Hugh	Weasel. Shiny whiskers, only two weeks in the womb and they wash themselves . . . more than you can say for human children, eh?

Clive	Suppose . . .
Hugh	Mm?
Clive	Suppose we had a human child *and* a weasel child.
Hugh	Well, it's up to you, but to be honest with you, Mr Dont, human children take a long time to gestate in the womb and cause the mother a lot of pain, unlike a weasel which pops out quick as anything.
Imelda	Hence 'pop goes the weasel'.
Hugh	Right. No, the easiest thing if you want a human child, is to buy one, ready-born, from a pet shop.
Imelda	I'll do it then. I'll give birth to a weasel and we'll buy a human child to keep it company.
Hugh	Fine. Any other questions?
Clive	Just one.
Hugh	Fire away.

Clive holds up the New Yorker.

Clive	Can you explain that cartoon?

Hugh looks at it for a while, puzzled.

VOX POP **Stephen** Road-widening scheme, I said. Road-widening scheme? Country-narrowing scheme more like. Yeah. Think about it. Country-narrowing scheme. Hm? Hmm?

Real Reality

Stephen addresses the camera.

Stephen Ladies and gentlemen, if you've been wearing your listening trousers at all over the last few time frames, it's not impossible that you will have heard the phrase Virtual Reality. You may have thought to yourself I *virtually* don't understand what that is, and even if I did, I *virtually* couldn't give a dalmatian's nephew. That's a shame. Because Virtual Reality represents a colossal leap forward in the field of computer-generated images. But we here on *A Bit of Fry & Laurie*, anxious as ever to bring you only the very ripest, tenderest young happening grooves, have looked ahead to the even more exciting field . . .

Hugh shouts, off camera.

Hugh And it is a field . . .
Stephen . . . and as m'colleague has so loudly pointed out, it is a field – the field of Real Reality. Hugh, what is it?

Hugh is wearing a brightly coloured tie. He sports it for the camera.

Hugh It's very exciting, that's what it is. This little beauty I'm wearing is a Real Reality Tie.

Stephen shouts across.

Stephen Cripes. What does that do?
Hugh What this does is enable me to stand here and experience everything around me exactly, but exactly, as if it was real. I can see people and lights and cameras, and m'colleague Stephen, all utterly indistinguishable from the real thing. I actually tried it out at home yesterday morning, and drank a cup of tea wearing this tie, and . . .
Stephen Did it taste just like a cup of tea?
Hugh Stephen, I swear I couldn't have told the difference. Then I went to Morocco, and crossed the Atlas mountains without ropes of any kind, and it really was pretty scary. It had me fooled, anyway.
Stephen Have you had sex while wearing it?
Hugh Very briefly, yes.
Stephen Identical, then?
Hugh No difference at all. I suppose the only criticism I have is that when you're wearing the tie, you're vaguely conscious of wearing a tie. Apart from that, it's as good as perfect.

Stephen	But what about the cost, Hugh? Surely that must be a worry?
Hugh	'Fraid so. This tie will set you back £475,000. But the manufacturers are hoping to produce a budget version sometime next year.
Stephen	Mmm. Can't wait. What are you going to do now, Hugh?
Hugh	I'm going to wear the tie in the next sketch.
Stephen	I am on the point of orgasm.

VOX POP Stephen *(as woman)* The local pizza delivery boy came round and I took one look and I said, never mind the super supreme, I'll take you, just as you are . . . thin and crispy. That's how we met. You could have knocked me down with a court order when I discovered he was my son.

Barman

Stephen is a barman. Hugh is leaning against the bar. He drains a glass.

Hugh	I'll have another one please, barman.
Stephen	Are you sure?
Hugh	*(aggressively)* What?
Stephen	No offence, but this'll be your seventh.
Hugh	Just keep 'em coming.
Stephen	OK, OK – your funeral.

Stephen takes out a glass, fills it with Ribena and adds water.

Hugh	Bitch.
Stephen	Come again?
Hugh	My wife.
Stephen	Ah, right.
Hugh	She doesn't understand me. She's never understood me.
Stephen	What, Polish or something is she?
Hugh	Have you ever been trapped in a loveless marriage with a woman you despised?
Stephen	Hoo, not since I was nine. Do you like it straight up, sir?
Hugh	Huh?
Stephen	Or with ice?
Hugh	Ice.

Stephen pushes drink to Hugh.

Stephen	Cocktail onion?
Hugh	No thanks. She takes no interest in my friends, she laughs at my ...
Stephen	Peanuts?
Hugh	... hobbies. No thanks. She doesn't even value my ...
Stephen	Crinkle-cut Cheesy Wotsit?

Stephen pushes a bowl of crinkle-cut Cheesy Wotsits towards Hugh, who takes one and chews it absent-mindedly.

Hugh	... career. Thanks. You know, I mean it's just so depressing. Alright so other men have got larger ...
Stephen	Plums?

Hugh waves away a bowl of plums. Stephen comes round to Hugh's side to do some wiping down and arranging of the bar-stools.

Hugh	. . . salaries and other men have got better cars and better prospects and more can boast a healthier . . .
Stephen	Stool?
Hugh	. . . lifestyle . . . ta . . .

Hugh sits, Stephen goes round.

	. . . alright, so I don't have that much cash lying around. But why complain? Others are worse off. I've got a job. I've got two sweet rosy . . .
Stephen	Nibbles?

A bowl of crisps is handed forward.

Hugh	. . . children. But she's always going on and on at me about my appearance. It's not as if she's an oil painting. I mean frankly she's . . .
Stephen	*(pointing at the crisps)* Plain and prawn flavoured.
Hugh	. . . not as young as she used to be herself. I don't know why I bother with women. I'd be better off being a . . .
Stephen	Fruit?
Hugh	. . . monk or a hermit or something. At least if I was a . . .
Stephen	Fag?
Hugh	. . . monk I wouldn't have to put up with women who can talk the back legs off a . . .
Stephen	Camel?
Hugh	Donkey. Of course the trouble is I couldn't live without women. In a monastery the best you can hope for is a bit of . . .
Stephen	Chocolate hob nob?
Hugh	. . . bit of spirituality and peace. And let's face it, we haven't slept together for years. I'm lucky if I get a bit of . . .
Stephen	Savoury finger?
Hugh	. . . a cuddle at Christmas. And naturally she won't let me give her so much as a . . .
Stephen	*(looking over his shoulder)* Good juicy tongue in the back passage.
Hugh	. . . peck on the cheek. The trouble with that woman is, she's just a . . .
Stephen	Rather disgusting-looking tart that should have been disposed of ages ago?
Hugh	. . . complainer.

Bangs his empty glass down.

	. . . One more for the road I think, barman.
Stephen	Anything to go with it?

Long pause.

Hugh	A bag of oral sex, if you've got one.

Karaoke

Stephen and Hugh are in a sort of limbo area, wearing stupid wigs.

Stephen	Hello. On the show tonight, I'm joined by a complex network of muscle tissue and tendons, controlled by my central nervous system. But I'm lucky enough to have as a guest Mr Philip Follip, who I believe has a remarkable invention. Hello, Philip.
Hugh	Hello, Riversdale.
Stephen	Alan.
Hugh	Oh. I'm sorry.
Stephen	I know it's spelt Riversdale, but it's actually pronounced 'Alan'.
Hugh	Alan it is then.
Stephen	Tell us about your invention, Philip, taking care not to be dull for a single moment.
Hugh	Well, basically, I looked at the karaoke machine, that's been such a popular hit over the last few years, and thought to myself how could I improve on it?
Stephen	Conclusions, Philip? You must have reached some, surely?
Hugh	Well, I thought the trouble with the karaoke machine is that it only allows you to sing along with it.
Stephen	Right, and you thought 'Hello, there's a window of opportunity, let's heave a brick through it.' Am I warm?
Hugh	Warm enough.
Stephen	That's all I ask.
Hugh	So I thought, what about a machine that would not only allow you to sing along with it, but would allow you to play along with it as well?
Stephen	I'm beginning to see how your mind works.
Hugh	And I came up with this.

Holds up a little black box with a button on it.

Stephen	I don't know if our cameras can see that ... If they can't, I suggest we take them back to the shop and get a fucking refund.
Hugh	If I just press this button here, then what happens is this ...

He presses the button and there is silence.

Stephen	Yes?
Hugh	Complete silence.
Stephen	Yes?

50

Hugh   Which now allows me and my orchestra to play and sing along.
One, two, three, four . . .

Cut wide to see full band: Hugh sings.

VOX POP **Hugh** Course, it's well known that Shakespeare didn't really exist. And that if he did, he was lots of people. And they were all women, and that all his plays were written by Alan Bleasdale. And that Shakespeare shot Kennedy, and that Lee Harvey Oswald was nothing but a pansy. They don't put that on *Newsnight*, though, do they?

Sophisticated Song

Hugh strums a piano.

Hugh

I wear sophisticated clothes,
I say sophisticated things,
Everything about me,
Says I'm a sophistication king,
But when I'm with you,
I can't seem to find my cool,
Yeah when I'm with you,
I just sit there and drool,

I got sophisticated hands,
I got sophisticated feet,
A sophisticated car,
Parked on sophistication street,
But when I'm with you,
I can't seem to find my cool,
Yeah when I'm with you,
I'm just a dribblin' fool,

And when you look at me,
And you start to flirt,
I have to wipe the dribble,
Off the front of my shirt,
And when you ask me,
What's on my mind,
All I can think to answer is . . .
blubblybubbylyfawaah,

I eat sophisticated food,
I breathe sophisticated air,
Use a sophisticated comb
On my sophisticated hair,
But when I'm with you,
I can't seem to find my cool,
Yes when I'm with you,
I just fall off my . . .

Amazingly enough, Hugh falls off his stool.

Throughout the winter, Abja will eat nothing but sheep. With the arrival of the warm southerly winds, however, her tastes become broader. Merlyn Rees (back row, kneeling) survived to become Home Secretary.

Although price includes flights, hotels and car hire, the company are obliged to point out that the woman holding the ball is a 'local', and may not be there for the whole course of your stay.

Pip Bennett and the author trying out the greased Black Back on a Cumbrian river. Here, Pip has just cast to a known lie, and the fish has taken. (Our efforts were unsuccessful, however, and we had to beat the fish to death with some big sticks that Pip always carries in the back of his Volvo.)

To the delight of the home crowd, Sally Gunnell salvages British pride with a time of 41.39.07. Baroness Trumpington (left) finished a disappointing fourth.

Ordinary commercial carrots are not nearly strong enough for this task. The carrot shown here, being put through its paces by Mr Gary Davies, has a tungsten tip.

A classic 'lick-out'. Neither team may cross the line until the codge has been retrieved. (In 1974, Holkham and Tharrock licked out for a record twenty-seven days. The rules have since been altered.)

The Gloucester Gladiolus: early prototype. Despite the enchanting fragrance and colourful display, Luftwaffe fighters scored repeated successes against this early model. The petals were later replaced with wings and the strike rate rapidly improved.

For Some Reason Angry

Stephen addresses the camera while making, tossing and dressing a salad.
For some reason he is very angry, as if always suspecting that everyone is
laughing at him.

Stephen I was at the theatre two nights ago. The National ... *OUR* National theat ... our *Royal* National Theatre. I saw a play, yes alright it was only a play. Oh brilliant, so now I'm to be judged and whipped and mocked and scorned because it was only a play. Great. Thanks very much indeed. Alright, yes it was only a sod-buggering play. No, MacEnroe wasn't in it, nor Lendl or Noah or any of the big stars. So it wasn't stuffed with top names. Christ, what do you want from me? Hm? Hm? Hm? My God, I go, I at least bloody bother to get off my fat, wobbling, lardy, smelly, huge, festering carpet and actually go to the theatre and suddenly I'm Adolf Eichmann. Well I'm sorry but ... WHY WON'T THIS FRIGGING TOMATO SETTLE BLOODY DOWN!!! *(He is having trouble slicing a tomato.)* God! What is the earthly use of trying, just for once in your life, to make an honest salad, just trying, without help, without any other motive than love and an honest desire without the CRUDDING ARSING thing falling apart in your bloody hands. God! Anyway, I saw a play there, by Shakespeare as it happens. And I started thinking. Thinking about Shakespeare ...

 O damn and BLAST this cucumber ... why does it have to be like this ...

VOX POP **Hugh** I walked into a shop the other day. Bloody hurt, I can tell you.

Cigars

A Jermyn Street tobacconist's. Stephen is behind the counter, Hugh isn't.

Hugh	Good morning.
Stephen	I beg your pardon?
Hugh	I said good morning.
Stephen	Oh sir. You've not heard?
Hugh	Heard what?
Stephen	Oh sir.
Hugh	What?
Stephen	Sir, I think I am a generous man, and I will happily bear many things. Burdens, architectural down-loads, even perhaps on fine summer days, your children. But bad tidings, sir ... bad tidings are too much for an inelastic old fool, such as you are currently experiencing, even to bear.
Hugh	Bad tidings?
Stephen	Suffice to say he's expected to make a full recovery.
Hugh	Who is?
Stephen	Call Nick Ross.
Hugh	What?
Stephen	Call Nick Ross is doing as well as can be expected. Meanwhiletime, a nation can only hold its breath in silent prayer and reflect in its quieter moments that flu can be a horrible and a very beastly thing.
Hugh	Nick Ross has got flu?
Stephen	Call Nick Ross is, according to sources close to Call Nick Ross, ill with the flu, sir, yes. How callous and casually violent your airy description of the goodness of the morning now sounds in your ears.
Hugh	Right. I'd like to buy a box of cigars, please.
Stephen	Cigars, of course. For smoking?
Hugh	Well, yes.
Stephen	Well, yes. Well, yes. Did two finer words in our language ever join hands and creep nervously down the aisle of utterance than 'well, yes'? If they did, it was without the help of a reputable catering firm, of that I am absolutely tall.
Hugh	What else would I use cigars for?
Stephen	Sir, the thought flitted across my knees that you might be thinking of using cigars as a means of personal transport around the crowded streets of our city. They are small, manoeuvrable, easy to park, and use almost no petrol.
Hugh	But they don't move.
Stephen	Sir is quick and alive to the *single* disadvantage of cigars in this respect. They do not, as Winston Churchill himself would not have

	been ashamed to say, move.
Hugh	Well, no, I want to smoke them.
Stephen	Sir wants to smoke cigars. He wants to take them out of the box, singly or in threes, put them in his mouth lengthways and apply a flame to the furthest end. Do I misjudge my man so terribly? I think not.
Hugh	No, that's right.
Stephen	Does sir imagine that he will be in a dressed state of affairs when the mood of ensmokement descends?
Hugh	I beg your pardon?
Stephen	Will sir be sheathed in habiliments, I am in the rapidly-expanding business of wondering, or will he be allowing the breath of God to caress his flinty flanks unhindered by layers of silk and, oblique stroke or, corduroy?
Hugh	I will be dressed, yes.
Stephen	Sir will be dressed. Will he, in this consummately dressed state, be in the company of four young walls and a ceiling, or will he be starkly alone?
Hugh	Outside?
Stephen	I believe that the young Francis Bacon coined the term 'outside' to describe just such a state of exteriority as I have been fumbling to express.
Hugh	I doubt I'll be smoking outside.
Stephen	Let me reach down into my word bag once again and feel for fitting shapes and textures to pull out and surprise you with. Ah, my word-fingers close around 'dressed' and they sense the smooth outlines of 'inside'. Sir will be experiencing the fumal joys of his cigaroid pleasure-cocks while 'dressed' and while 'inside'. I HARDLY THINK I CAN PUT IT MORE PLAINLY THAN THAT.
Hugh	Forgive me for asking, but what on earth has it got to do with anything whether or not I'm inside or outside, nude or clothed?
Stephen	NUDE! 'Nude!' he said, smiting his brow with the back of his mind. Nude was the very word I could have used earlier. It would have saved us an hundred syllables of pointless and unutterably tedious exchange earlier on. Why did I not simply say, 'Will sir be nude?' My aunt and my cousin (a cinema projectionist in Hove, as was) will never forgive me.
Hugh	You haven't answered my question.
Stephen	I am now busy until the end of the month wondering if sir will allow me to answer his simple, manly question with one of my own?
Hugh	Oh, very well.
Stephen	You are kindness herself.
Hugh	Well?
Stephen	Sir?

Hugh	What is your question?
Stephen	Stand back to admire it, sir, because though I say so without an interpreter, it's the best question asked since man first arose from out the primordial cup-a-soup and asked 'What is the word for that tiny sleeve of plastic at the end of a shoe-lace?' My question is this and it comes without sponsorship of any kind: 'What are you doing here?'
Hugh	Well, I think I'm trying to buy some cigars.
Stephen	*Some*? Some cigars? Oh sir, that is the most vest-dampening attitude I have heard since Peter Lilley was in here, trying to buy my ...
Hugh	Trying to buy your?
Stephen	My silence, sir. You tell me you are trying to buy '*some* cigars'. This is not a shop that sells 'some cigars', this is a shop that sells only the very finest cigars that sexual favours can buy. Cigars that think, that feel: cigars that adjust themselves to your mood and your state of arousal.
Hugh	Are you saying that you sell different cigars for indoor and outdoor use and different cigars for being clothed or unclothed?
Stephen	No sir. I am emphatically not saying that. But I could. By God, with a fair following wind, a sip of Aqua Libra, a week's rehearsal and a nod from you, I could say exactly that.

VOX POP **Hugh** I like a nice bit of fresh sleep. Not like that tinned stuff.

Don't be Dirty

Stephen is a genial afternoon game show host. He is flanked by Hugh and Clive.

Stephen   Hello, and welcome to *Don't be Dirty*, the show that shows you don't have to be dirty. With us is Tony, three times semi-finalist, and Clive, keen to be clean, who got through unexpectedly when last week's winner, Mr Nottingham, died in a canoe. Tony, you to start. Will you please describe for us the act of fellatio, Tony – the act of fellatio – without, Tony, without, and I'm sure you must know the rules by now, without being dirty. Your time starts five seconds ago.

'Fellatio' flashes up on the screen.

Hugh   This is an act, an act that takes place between two people, possibly of opposite sexes, but possibly not...

Stephen   Oooh, careful, Tony...

Hugh   ... whereby one of the participants takes a part of the other participant's person into the place where they might more commonly keep bubble gum, say, and proceeds to masticate...

Stephen   Oooh, Tony, I thought you'd gone there. You're playing with fire, man...

Hugh   ... until the other participant arrives at a state of pleasurable relaxation. The second participant then gives the first participant ten quid and goes back home.

A gong sounds.

Stephen   Unbelievable. Can no one beat the big man from Hunstanton? Clive, it's up to you. Your topic is the preservation of hard woods, and your time starts ... then.

'The Preservation of Hard Woods' flashes up.

Clive   Well, this is a very necessary business...

A buzzer sounds.

Stephen   Tony's challenged...
Hugh   Business.
Stephen   Business, yes, you did say it, Clive. Little bit dirty, there, one point away, but plenty of time to go.

Clive	... operation that has to be carried out if developers are not to rase your hard woods to the ground and ...

Hugh buzzes again.

Stephen	Another challenge from our reigning champion. The nature of your challenge, Tony, please.
Hugh	He said 'rase'.
Stephen	He did say 'rase', Tony.
Hugh	Rase is an anagram of arse.

Clive is furious with himself.

Stephen	Rase *is* an anagram of arse, it is, it is, it is. So sorry Clive, but we do have to lose you. You were Keen to be Clean, but you came up against a man very much on the top of his form. We say goodbye.
Clive	Oh, piss.
Stephen	Now, Tony, you've been in this position before. You *keep* the *Don't be Dirty* Sweatshop and Neck, you *keep* the 800 pounds in weight. They're yours to keep. No one can take them away from you. AS OF RIGHT, they are yours and yours alone. If anyone touches them or tries to appropriate them you would be justified in taking extreme and violent measures of self-protection. But, I'm offering you now 600 more pounds or a chance to go into another *Don't be Dirty* Daily Double with a chance to win ten pounds.
Hugh	I'll go for the daily double.
Stephen	I knew you'd say that, Tony. You're a sport, quite a sport. But do remember you KEEP the prizes you've already won. They're yours. No one else's. Yours. You're clear on that?
Hugh	I'm clear, Bradley.
Stephen	Alright. So long as that's clear. They're yours to keep. Yours. Now. Can we have our *Don't be Dirty* Daily Double categories on the board, please? Your three categories are (*as they come up on the big board*) 'rimming', 'genital torture' and 'David Vine'.
Hugh	Ooh.
Stephen	Remember it is a Daily Double, so *two* subjects. I must hurry you as you take your time. Just take your time, very quickly.
Hugh	Hard. It's very hard. I think 'genital torture' and 'David Vine' please.

Lights go down. Stephen suddenly gets very quiet and serious.

Stephen	Tony. You have thirty earth seconds in which to talk about genital torture and David Vine without being dirty and your thirty seconds start ...

Stephen looks at his wristwatch.

. . . damn – missed that one – coming up. Coming up. Your thirty
seconds start – *now*!

Hugh   A certain class of person exists who derives some kind of undefined
pleasure in inflicting quite excruciating pain upon the parts of their
bodies which are designed to be hidden inside pants and vests. To this
end nipple-clamps and scrotal compressors are deployed, as well as a
variety of serrated needles which can be inserted down the channels
and pipe-work which constitute the organs of generation. Presenting
various sporting events, most especially the world snooker finals from the
Crucible Theatre, Sheffield, David Vine combines relaxed and informative
presentational skills with a clear expertise on the game. He . . .

Claxon sounds.

Stephen   Oh Tony. Tony, Tony, Tony. 'On the game'! You said 'on the
game'. You were dirty, Tony and that's a pity.

Hugh hits his head.

Hugh   I *was* dirty. I *was* dirty. Shite-arsed damn.
Stephen   Only four seconds left and you were dirty. Well, David Vine was
obviously going to be a category which could trip up even a seasoned
Don't be Dirty finalist like yourself. I'm afraid you lose the prizes you've
won this week, and everything from the weeks before. You repay to us
your travel expenses and you go away empty-headed. You knew the
risks.
Hugh   I did. I did.
Stephen   But Tony, tell me. Did you enjoy yourself? Has it been a pleasure?
Hugh   It's been a huge one, a really big one. I've pleasured myself a great deal.
Stephen   I'm glad to hear it. Until next week, ladies and gentlemen. And remember.
Both   Don't be dirty!

Interruptus

Imelda is washing up at a kitchen sink. Stephen comes in. It's a little bit EastEnders *and a little bit* The Archers *and a little bit other things too.*

Stephen	Julie . . .
Imelda	Hello, Frank. Kettle's on.
Stephen	Thanks, love. Julie, there's something I wanted to tell you . . .
Imelda	Can't it wait? Only I've got to pick Rebecca up at four.
Stephen	Well no, it can't really . . .
Imelda	Make it quick.
Stephen	I'm trying . . .
Imelda	Only I've got to pick Rebecca up at four.
Stephen	Well it's not easy. Thing is . . .
Imelda	Blimey, it's nearly four now. I've got to pick Rebecca up in a minute.
Stephen	Hold on. This is important . . .
Imelda	Important?
Stephen	Yeah. You see . . .

The door opens and Clive comes in.

Imelda	Bill . . .
Clive	Sorry, am I . . . ?
Imelda	No, it's alright. Frank was just going to tell me something important, but I've got to pick Rebecca up at four, so . . .
Clive	I'll pick Rebecca up, if you like.
Imelda	Are you sure?
Clive	Yeah, no problem. What time?
Imelda	Four . . .
Clive	Blimey, it's nearly four now . . .
Imelda	I know . . .
Clive	I'll go and pick her up, then.
Imelda	Kettle's on . . .
Clive	No, it's alright. Better get a move on if I'm going to make it by four . . .
Imelda	Thanks.
Clive	See ya.

Clive goes out.

Imelda	Now then. What's so important?
Stephen	Well . . .
Imelda	Kettle's on, by the way . . .

Stephen	No thanks.
Imelda	Sure? Won't take a minute.
Stephen	No, really ... Julie, you and I ...

Clive comes back in.

Clive	Sorry ...
Imelda	What's wrong? Is Rebecca alright?
Clive	Fine, fine ...
Imelda	Tell me what's happened ...
Clive	Nothing's happened. It's just ...
Imelda	What?
Clive	Where am I picking her up from?
Imelda	Rebecca?
Clive	Yeah ...
Imelda	Tony's.
Clive	Tony's, right. What time?
Imelda	Well I said four ...
Clive	Blimey, I'd better get a move on ...
Imelda	Thanks.

Clive goes out again.

	Now then. What about that tea?
Stephen	No thanks ...
Imelda	Sure? Kettle's on ...
Stephen	No. Look, Julie ...
Imelda	Two seconds. Warm the pot, couple of tea bags ...
Stephen	Julie ...
Imelda	What?
Stephen	Thanks, I'd love a cup.

Imelda pours some tea.

Imelda	So, this big important thing that can't wait ...
Stephen	Yeah, well. I don't know how to put this ...
Imelda	Just say it.
Stephen	It's not that easy. The thing is ...
Imelda	Sugar?
Stephen	Two, please. Julie, you and I have known each other a long time, yeah?
Imelda	Yeah.
Stephen	I s'pose, what I'm trying to say is ...

The door opens and Hugh enters.

Hugh	Have either of you seen Bill?
Imelda	Bill?
Hugh	Yeah. He was supposed to be giving me a lift…
Imelda	He's gone to fetch Rebecca…
Hugh	What time?
Imelda	Five.
Hugh	Five?
Imelda	No, wait a minute, four.
Hugh	Four?
Imelda	Four.
Hugh	Sure?
Imelda	Sure. He'll be back in a minute.
Hugh	Oh, I'll hang on then. You haven't got the kettle on, have you?
Imelda	No, kettle's off.

VOX POP **Stephen** Damnedest thing. I was in this hardware shop the other day, buying a thirty gallon drum of car wax for my daughter-in-law, when the door bursts open, thirty coppers come lumbering in, and arrest everyone. Place turned out to be a brothel. Quite unbelievable. I mean it said Brothel outside it, but I just thought that was a joke.

Soccer School

Stephen in sheepskin coat, standing on the edge of a football pitch, addresses the camera.

Stephen   You're a parent. You have children. You want those children to become Premier League footballers. Well, this is the place for you. The Dave Wilson School in Ipswich, in the heart of London's East End.

A line of ten-year-old boys are doing physical jerks. A track-suited Hugh gives instructions as Stephen's voice continues.

The name of Dave Wilson will be familiar to anyone who knows him. And also to those who followed the fortunes of Reading Town reserves during the dark days of the seventies.

Close-up on Hugh.

Hugh   They were very dark days, yes. Very dark. Hmm. I hadn't thought of them as dark, but now you mention it...

Stephen   Dave played a total of two games for the side before a cartilege snapped in his head. Dave. What was it like, to be thrown out on the scrap-heap at such a young age? Did you feel bitter?

Hugh   Ooh no. Worse if anything.

Stephen   No, *bitter.*

Hugh   Oh. Yeah. Bitter. Bitter ... and dark ... days.

Cut to Hugh leading some stretching exercises. Stephen in voice-over.

Stephen   Following the injury, Dave tried his hand at many things. Nightclub owner, astrologer, interior designer, Shadow Home Secretary, the jobs came and went, but nothing seemed to stick. Until Dave turned up one day to watch his nephew playing in the school side.

Hugh   I wanted to get involved. That's it, really. You know, football has been good to me, and I suppose I saw the chance to put something back into the game.

Cut to the boys listening as Hugh lectures them.

Football is a very simple game. What is it?

Boys   A very simple game.

Hugh   What is the object of the game of football?

Boys	Run into the box and fall over.
Hugh	Run into the box and fall over. Right. Ricky, off you go.

The boys form a line and one by one they run to the penalty area and dive spectacularly to the ground, clutching their shins. Cut to interview.

Hugh	I'm trying to teach fundamental footballing skills at the earliest possible age. I've started teaching my eight-month-old son to fall over, and I've got to say, the lad's a natural. Falls over like a diamond.
Stephen	You think he might follow in his father's footsteps?
Hugh	Yes. For a while. But then, with a bit of luck, he'll fall over.

Hugh demonstrates technique.

Got to get your head back. As you go. Keep the neck loose, as you approach the box, then . . .

Hugh throws himself down.

Got it? Right. Limping. Two lengths of the pitch. Go.

The boys set off in massively exaggerated limps. Hugh approaches Stephen.

See that lad there?

Close-up on a boy, limping spectacularly.

Hugh	Kid's got a future. No doubt about it. We've had a couple of London clubs down to look at him already. Falls like a dream, and he can limp just as well with either foot.
Stephen	Shouting at the referee?
Hugh	Let's have a look. Daniel?

The boy turns.

I'm the ref.

Boy	Oh, but I've already . . .
Hugh	You want to make it to the top or don't you?

Daniel shambles over and starts yelling at Hugh, nose to nose. Hugh turns to Stephen.

He's something, isn't he?

Another boy approaches Stephen and Hugh carrying a football.

Boy	Mr Wilson?
Hugh	Martin.
Boy	Found this in the changing-room.
Hugh	Oh yeah?
Boy	What is it?
Hugh	Never you mind about that.

Hugh takes the ball and shouts to all the boys.

Hugh   Right, listen! Martin found this in the changing-room. Now I'm going to say this once. I don't want any of you wasting your time with these things. Any of you see one of these, you tell me or Mr Collins immediately. You want to make it to the League, then you think about training. No one ever got to the top of the game mucking around with these things, alright?

Hugh makes to punt the ball away, but misses.
    Cut to Stephen standing in front of a sign reading 'The Dave Wilson Falling Over School'.

Stephen   Hope for the future, then.

VOX POP Hugh I grew up in what would now be considered rather a stern family, I suppose. My father wouldn't have a television in the house, so we used to gather round every night and watch it on the lawn.

Golf

Hugh and Caroline are at a table, having tea with their son Terry, ten years old.

Caroline	Something wrong, dear?
Terry	Nah.
Caroline	You're not eating your tea.
Terry	Not hungry.
Hugh	Watch it.
Terry	What?
Hugh	Not hungry. Jesus.
Terry	Can't I have an apple?
Hugh	No you can't.
Terry	But...
Hugh	But? But? No buts in this house, my lad. In this house, we leave our buts outside, where they belong. Alright?
Caroline	Eat some of your Pepsi-flavoured chocolate crisps, dear, and then we'll see about apples...

The door bell goes. Caroline gets up and goes out.

Hugh	Not hungry.
Terry	Well I'm not...
Hugh	I'll decide whether you're hungry or not, thank you very much for cleaning my car.

The door opens and Caroline comes in with Patrick.

Caroline	Mr Furkiss, father.
Patrick	Hello.
Hugh	I see, I see. Can he state his business, this Mr Furkiss, or is he going to stand there all night like an over-filled bin-liner?
Caroline	Father...
Hugh	I speak as I find, Mr Furkiss. You'll realise that, as you get to know me. Now then. What's on your mind you wide-arsed git?
Caroline	At least let the man sit down, father.
Hugh	Mr Furkiss can do his talking standing up, mother. We had to, at his age.
Patrick	Well now, I'm glad that Terry's here for this...
Hugh	Well where else would he be, eh? Tea-time on a Wednesday. Ram-raiding old ladies in the High Street, is that what you think?
Patrick	Not at all...
Hugh	I should think not at all...
Caroline	Mr Furkiss is from the school, father. He teaches Terry's form.

A pause and then Hugh jumps to his feet

Hugh	Mr Furkiss, for goodness' sake sit down. Will you take some tea with us? Mother, freshen this tea-pot up with fresh tea, will you? Mr Furkiss teaches at Patrick's school...
Patrick	No tea, thank you.
Hugh	Pepsi-flavoured chocolate crisp?
Patrick	Well perhaps a little one...
Hugh	Mother, fetch up the littlest crisp you can find, and some of our smallest cutlery to go with it.

Caroline busies herself.

	Now then, Mr Furkiss, will you take a pipe of rough shag with me over here by the radiator?
Patrick	Thank you, no. I really came to discuss Terry's progress at school.
Hugh	He's not been making progress, has he? The little bugger. That lad'll feel the rough end of my watch strap before the day is over, Mr Furkiss, you have my word on it.
Patrick	Well no, actually, he's not been making any progress. That's why I'm here.
Hugh	Hello? Mother, this sounds like bad news...
Caroline	Just tell us, Mr Furkiss. Terry's no angel, we realise that. If he's done wrong, we'd like to know about it.
Patrick	The truth is, Terry has been falling further and further behind with his golf.
Hugh	Golf?
Caroline	Golf?
Patrick	As you know, he's got exams coming up at the end of this year, and I fear that Terry is going to fail his golf unless he bucks his ideas up pretty smartly.
Hugh	I don't believe it...
Patrick	I'm afraid it's true.
Caroline	But golf was always his strongest subject. He came top in golf last year...
Patrick	Exactly. That's why I wanted to come here, have a little chat, see if I couldn't find out what's been happening.
Hugh	I don't understand it. We thought...

Patrick produces some cards.

Patrick	These are the score cards from his last three rounds, Mr Furkiss. As you can see, he shot an eighty-four last Wednesday, and a ninety this morning.

Hugh examines the cards.

Hugh	Bloody Nora. An eight on the fourteenth? Eight? That's pathetic.
Patrick	It is disappointing, I agree.
Caroline	The fourteenth is the one...
Patrick	It's the dog-leg par four. Couple of sand traps, but well out of harm's way.
Hugh	Two hundred and twelve yards from the medal tee. It's a piece of cake.
Patrick	The rest of the form managed a six or better, and so you can imagine why I was concerned...
Hugh	Terry, you little bugger...
Caroline	Don't shout at him, father...
Hugh	I shout as I find, as you well know, mother.
Patrick	Terry? What's happening? Is there something bothering you?
Terry	No.
Patrick	Are you sure? Nothing you'd like to tell me about?
Terry	No.
Hugh	Answer Mr Furkiss, Terry. He's come a long way on a dark afternoon for your benefit...
Terry	There's nothing wrong.
Caroline	Well then why, Terry? Why an eight on the fourteenth?
Hugh	He did it to spite us, can't you see? All the sacrifices we made, and he's throwing it back in our faces. He's an evil little bastard, that's what he is.
Terry	I'm not, I just...
Stephen	You just what, Terry?
Terry	Nothing.
Patrick	You're slicing the ball much more than you used to. Why is that? Left hand too far over?
Hugh	Cocks his wrists too early. I've always said it...
Caroline	Hush, father...
Hugh	Well he does, no getting round it...
Terry	I just...
Stephen	Yes?
Terry	I just don't see the point, that's all.
Hugh	Don't see the point? Don't see the point of what?
Terry	Of golf.
Hugh	Don't see the... That's nice, isn't it? Your mother and I have sweated and sweated and sweated for you. We've sweated so much it's disgusting. Tell him, mother. Tell him how much you've sweated. Show him the stains on your blouse.
Caroline	*(pointing)* There.
Hugh	You'd better start pulling your ideas up, my boy. What are you going to do with your life if you fail golf, hm? What kind of prospects do you think there are out there for people who cock their wrists too early?

Terry	I came top in French, didn't I?
Hugh	French? French? I'll French you, young man.
Caroline	No you won't, Father.
Hugh	French, indeed.
Patrick	The national curriculum is about the real world, Terry.
Hugh	*(examining reports)* Bottom in golf. Bottom in Sonic Two. Bottom in Lemmings. Bottom in Disney studies. But when it comes to something cushy and of no practical use whatever . . . mathematics, French, English . . .
Caroline	Oh Terry . . .
Hugh	So. A new regime for you, young man. It's the driving range and practice greens with every hour of daylight God sends. And in the evenings you will practise your Sonic Two and your Lemmings and you will study your Disney videos.
Terry	But . . .
Hugh	Uh . . . what did I tell you about buts? We do not bring our buts into the tea-lounge.
Terry	Mum promised I could go to the library this evening.
Hugh	Well, you should have thought of that before you started slicing the ball off the tee and shanking your approaches, shouldn't you? Now. Go inside and watch *Bedknobs and Broomsticks*.

Hugh looks as Terry slouches off.

Caroline	Don't you worry, Mr Furkiss, we'll keep an eye on him.
Patrick	Oh good. He's a nice lad, Terry, be nice to see him get on in life.
Hugh	Now then. What about that rough shag?

Head Gardener

Stephen is at home in his bathroom, bent over a sink, washing his hair. He hums and washes. He spots the camera.

Stephen   Hello. If you're anything like me then you probably wash your hair quite often and you probably use a shampoo. You're pretty tall, you're called Stephen and you haven't got much time for gardening. Well, I may have just the answer for you, Stephen. It came to me yesterday, when I was standing here bent over the wash hair basin. Here's a thing we do a couple of times a week (though if it's more than that I urge you to consider the benefits of a specially formulated frequency shampoo) and which utilises the very same key nutrients and minerals that any gardener will tell you are essential for healthy plants and gums. So, Stephen, I've come up with this new five-minute addition to my hair grooming and facial scrub programme. If you're anything like me you'll probably like to rinse after your second wash and you'll have a friend called Hugh who plays with an Etch-a-Sketch in your airing cupboard.

Stephen opens the airing cupboard where Hugh is sitting and Etch-a-Sketching.

Stephen   Hugh, come on out and help me explain my new break-through in hair.

Hugh   Right-o.

Stephen   I was explaining to the viewing several that after the second wash I like to have a thorough rinse.

Hugh   No harm in that, if it's done sensibly.

Stephen   Exactly my point. And it's at this stage when my new development comes in. Here, in my freshly-watered, protein-enriched hair are the ideal conditions – neutral balance Ph, active liposomes and gentle cleansing agents – for a small, but attractive town-garden. Hugh.

Hugh takes a packet of seeds and starts to plop them in Stephen's hair.

Stephen   What have you chosen, Hugh?

Hugh   A mix of begonias, dog-roses and clematis.

Stephen   No vegetables?

Hugh   I thought perhaps I could sow one or two potatoes just behind the crown here.

Stephen   So a general utility garden.

Hugh   Pretty much.

Stephen   Well. Now I have to blow-dry with my Pifco tress-matic on its lowest setting and let nature do its work.

Time has passed. Stephen now has a towel over his head.

Well, let's see how it's fared.

Hugh removes towel to show spectacular garden. Flowers, patch of lawn, rockery . . . the works.

Hugh   I think that's come out rather well.
Stephen   Simple cheap, effective. Well done Hugh, my head gardener.
Hugh   That's amusing.
Stephen   *(to camera)* Of course your own hair garden needn't be confined to this limited range of plants. The sky's very much the limit. Climbing wistarias, alpines, runner beans, you name it. And if you have dandruff problems you might consider a traditional Japanese snow garden.
Hugh   If you're anything like me, you'll be keen to experiment and you will enjoy wearing lycra one-pieces alone in your bedroom.

Stephen goes and stands oddly, looking at a wall.

What are you doing Stephen?
Stephen   I'm south facing.
Hugh   *(picking up Etch-a-Sketch)* Ah, well it's back to the airing cupboard for me.
Stephen   See you next wash day.
Both   Ber-bye.

VOX POP **Stephen** I think the Queen does a ruddy marvellous job. Ruddy marvellous. I opened Parliament myself a couple of times in the seventies, and believe you me, it's not as easy as it looks.

Red and Shiny

In the street, Stephen addresses the camera.

Stephen   It's red, it's shiny, it's instantly desirable and it's remarkably cheap. One drawback. It doesn't exist yet. We wondered why not. Douglas Hurd has been foreign secretary for a record five years. If anyone knows it'll be Gordon Wade of Market Soundings plc.

Hugh is there as Gordon.

Gordon. It's red, it's shiny – everyone wants one, it needn't cost a fortune and it isn't tested on animals. Yet it doesn't exist. What's going on?

Hugh   I don't know. We're very sorry. It should exist, I know that. Believe me we're working on it.

Stephen   Have you thought of a name for it yet?

Hugh   Not as of yet, no. The project has a working title . . .

Stephen   I've just got time to ask you, what is it?

Hugh   The name at this moment is Mark Bannister.

Stephen   Mark Bannister. Price?

Hugh   We're hoping it'll be round about three pounds fifty, but it may go as high as ninety thousand.

Stephen   Ninety thousand?

Hugh   Rather depends on what it does, you see. And how much it costs to make it. But these are details . . .

Stephen   Exactly. The basic message is, you're going ahead, and we might expect to see Mark Bannisters in our shops soon? Fair answer.

Dalliard: Piano

Hugh enters a shop. There are pianos about the place. Stephen is ready.

Hugh	Hello.
Stephen	It does seem to be, sir, yes.
Hugh	Seem to be what?
Stephen	Rather hello.
Hugh	Sorry?
Stephen	I opened my television last night only to find that nice gentleman with the legs advancing the prediction that it might be rather 'good evening' today, but looking out through the window that the previous owners thoughtfully installed for the purpose, I find that it has, as you athletically observed, turned out to be rather 'hello'.
Hugh	Mmm. Nice weather.
Stephen	And a very nice weather to you too, sir. *(Calling off.)* We have a customer, Mr Dalliard! It's pleasantly spoken but with a loud taste in vests. I'm talking to it now. *(To Hugh.)* Sir. How can I make your life more attractively-styled?
Hugh	Well now, it is my god-daughter's birthday next week, and she's very keen to have a piano.
Stephen	I understand, absolutely, sir. I have god-daughters of my own.
Hugh	Yes, well . . .
Stephen	You would like me to bundle her into a large trunk and transport her to the continent of Africa, where she might join the slave trade and become a lasting credit to you and your collection of hand-painted Chinese rugs?
Hugh	Well . . . no.
Stephen	No?
Hugh	No.
Stephen	No in the sense of 'Yes, and is it alright if I pay by cheque?'
Hugh	No, no in the sense of 'no'.
Stephen	Hmm. I fear that being with you is one of the accomplishments I have yet to master in my short, but interestingly shaped life. *(Calling off.)* Things are turning frosty, Mr Dalliard.
Hugh	I'd like to buy a piano.
Stephen	For your god-daughter?
Hugh	For my god-daughter.
Stephen	With what end in view?
Hugh	So that she can learn to play it.
Stephen	With what end of the piano in view, you blithering customer?
Hugh	Er . . . both ends, I think . . .

Stephen	A double-ended piano?
Hugh	Yes.
Stephen	*(calling)* Mr Dalliard! A situation is developing! *(To Hugh.)* How old is this so-called god-daughter of yours?
Hugh	Seventeen.
Stephen	Mr Dalliard! Stop your ears, the talk is becoming loose. Seventeen and you want to buy her a piano.
Hugh	Yes.
Stephen	For your god-daughter?
Hugh	Is there a problem?
Stephen	I wouldn't go so far as Reading, sir. Although they tell me that it's in Berkshire at this time of year.
Hugh	Look. I came in here . . .
Stephen	So far, sir, I am in complete agreement with you. You came in here. You bloody . . . well . . . came . . . in . . . here. You did. If you hadn't come in here, I would have noticed, and called the Church of England immediately. But you did come in here, and here you stand, proud, slightly lopsided, the finest full-page advertisement for the Anglo-Saxon race I've seen since yesterday's edition of *Brookside*.
Hugh	I want to buy a piano.
Stephen	We all want to buy pianos, sir.
Hugh	Do we?
Stephen	Leaving aside the vast majority of human beings who don't want to buy pianos, yes sir.
Hugh	So?
Stephen	Mr Dalliard! Start your ears again. This is getting exciting. *(To Hugh.)* Sir, you are, you have been, you were, you are, you did, you always will be, the master of that sixty-foot gaff-rigged schooner that plies the oceans of the world in the name of 'Your Destiny', but might I recommend that you take at least one shagging moment to think about this?
Hugh	What?
Stephen	God-daughters are not horses, sir.
Hugh	No . . .
Stephen	Neither are they commercial aircraft, nor streets of terraced housing in what used to be called Hull.
Hugh	No . . .
Stephen	They are not quantities of tepid water that collect in the bottom of up-turned tea-cups during the wash cycle, no more are they hard-boiled sparrows.
Hugh	Your point being?
Stephen	I have no point sir. I am, to all in tents and caravans, pointless.
Hugh	Right. One piano, please.
Stephen	Very well, sir. I have strained every groin I have to dissuade you from

	your chosen course of action. You will realise that I am too proud to beg, and too tall to sit comfortably in a Lotus Seven. If, as I surmise, sir has the bit between his teeth well and truly between his teeth, there is nothing more I can do without using Venn diagrams and multi-coloured flow charts.
Hugh	One ... piano ... please.

Stephen reaches beneath the counter and produces a vibrator.

Stephen	That'll be twenty-nine of your earth pounds and ninety-five pence please Bob.
Hugh	That's a vibrator.
Stephen	Sir?
Hugh	That is a vibrator.
Stephen	I realise that, sir. I am not entirely French.
Hugh	I don't want a vibrator.
Stephen	You've changed your mind? *(Calling.)* Mr Dalliard! Unpack the suitcases at once. The young git has changed his mind ...
Hugh	No, I haven't changed my mind. I never wanted a vibrator. I wanted a piano.
Stephen	Perhaps you are not a native of these shores, sir.
Hugh	What's that got to do with it?
Stephen	Or perhaps you merely thought, the grouse and the partridge being out of season, you could derive some sport from this humble shopkeeper, a man who palpably lives in Putney and grows other people's vegetables? Is that how your mind works?
Hugh	Look ...
Stephen	If that is what you thought, then I feel sorry for me. I may not be a duke or an ambassador's wife, but I know the price of a pound's worth of lard, and can recite the days of the week from memory.
Hugh	I just want a piano. Not a vibrator. A piano. For my god-daughter. For her birthday. So that she can play it. That's all I want. Alright? Will you sell me one, or will I have to go elsewhere?
Stephen	This time, sir, the dice has fallen in my favour. The worm has turned and the little man has his chance. Elsewhere will be closed.
Hugh	Closed?
Stephen	Closed. So now, your scheme is blown, shattered, it lies in pieces at your feet in a grotesque, mocking parody of local news broadcasts. You are a spent force, Mr Customer, yesterday's man, a speck on the pages of our island history. You are like a shoe-lace, looking for a nest. You are, in short, long.
Hugh	I don't know why, but I'm going to give you one last chance. Sell ... me ... a ... frigging ... piano.

Stephen	*(rapidly)* Upright, grand, boudoir grand, baby grand, concert grand?
Hugh	That's more like it. Upright.
Stephen	Cordless? With or without clitoral exciter?
Hugh	*(ominously)* What?
Stephen	Ivory-white, flesh pink, fluted or unfluted?

Hugh grabs Stephen by the lapels.

Hugh	Now, listen...
Stephen	Mr Dalliard! Step out at once, never mind your hat, and take an intensive course in self-defence. Come back when you have attained your fourth dan and give Mr Customer a thorough spanking.
Hugh	I don't want a vibrator. I'm not interested in vibrators. I want a piano. Do you understand?
Stephen	I read you, Mr Sir. I read you like a heart-warming tale of human courage and star-crossed love serialised in weekly instalments by the author of 'Danielle Steele's Emeralds'. Piano. One. God-daughter. Seventeen. For the use of.

Hugh lets go.

Hugh	Right. Now. Show me what you've got.
Stephen	Mr Dalliard! Ignore my previous instructions. The UN-inspired truce is holding. Sir and I are singing from the same song-sheet. Resume your carving. *(To Hugh: pointing at piano.)* May I urge the merits of this particular instrument upon you, sir? It is the Toyota Previa of pianos, the Radion Ultra of keyboards.

Hugh looks at it.

Hugh	Don't be ridiculous. It would never fit her.

VOX POP **Hugh** My father's advice, I'll never forget it – neither a borrower, nor a git be.

Gelliant Gutfright

Stephen sits in a leather armchair and addresses the camera, spookily and fast.

Stephen   Between imagination and desire, between reality and ambition, between what is known and what is feared, between purpose and despair, between sense and shite, between the visible world and the inner world that straddles the curtain hung between what we know and what we think we suspect is a dark veil that waves gently between the beckoning finger drawing us into the world of what could be and what never couldn't be impossible to dread. OR DO THEY? Perhaps it isn't. Maybe we were only dreaming? Perhaps the answers can be found in that other realm that lies between the foundry of the heart and the sweating laundry-room of the imagination where the only rhythms are the smiles of a forgotten winter and the incessant beating of the frightened human thigh that we call 'Fear'. Or is it? I'm Gelliant Gutfright and tonight's tale must give us pause. It is called 'Flowers For Wendy' but might it rather have been called 'You Have Been Warned'? No, it might not.

The picture starts to fade.

Andrew Beckett is on his way home from work. A nice young man is Andrew Beckett. A kind word for everyone and liked by all who come into contact with him.

We see a smiley Hugh walking along the street. He passes a flower stall, manned by a sinister looking Patrick, with dark glasses and white stick.

Stephen   *(now off)* Another hard day's work. Another quiet evening in. Perhaps a little television, the crossword. Maybe he'll finally get round to cataloguing those . . . wait!

Hugh stops and clicks his fingers as he remembers something.

What is he thinking of? Not just another evening, after all. It's Wendy's birthday! Dinner at Mario's! But first he should . . .

Hugh turns and sees the flower stall.

Strange! He's never noticed that stall before. Yet he comes home this way every evening . . . providential.

Hugh walks towards the flower stall.

Patrick	Good evening, Mr Beckett.
Hugh	(*amazed*) But that's extraordinary! How on earth do you know what time of day it is? You aren't wearing a watch.
Patrick	I know many things, Mr Beckett. Would you like to buy some flowers for your wife's birthday?
Hugh	This is uncanny! Flowers are *exactly* what I want. How could you possibly have known?

Patrick smiles creepily.

Patrick	How about some roses? All the ladies love a rose.

Hugh looks around. He sees some yellow things.

Hugh	What are these?
Patrick	Ah. You don't want those, Mr Beckett. Those are special blooms.
Hugh	They're rather fine. What are they called?
Patrick	Ranunculus pugnans.
Hugh	(*picking the bunch up*) Ranunc . . . what?
Patrick	Commonly known, sir, as Old Man's Wrinkle or the Fighting Buttercup.
Hugh	Well, I think they're lovely. The smell is . . .

Hugh sniffs deeply.

Patrick	They didn't get that name by accident, Mr Beckett.
Hugh	What name?
Patrick	The Fighting Buttercup. They say that the bouquet of this bloom will bring out all the anger in a person.
Hugh	Oh what nonsense.
Patrick	That's what they say.
Hugh	Superstitious hooey.
Patrick	No doubt you're right, sir.
Hugh	Arse-clap.
Patrick	As you say, sir.
Hugh	Rhino-bollocks. How much are they?
Patrick	Five pounds, sir. But I . . .

Hugh gives him a fiver and stalks off. Patrick watches him go. Hugh knocks over an old woman in the street as he goes.

   Cut to Hugh tutting as he tries to let himself into the flat. He mutters at the recalcitrance of the key.

Stephen	*(voice-over)* Poor Andrew. Poor Wendy. A kind thought for a birthday and a simple bunch of flowers. But when your life is a perilous yoyo, eaten by Destiny's right hand: when Fate lights the cigarette: when Chance plays the trumpet not very well and Hazard deals the cards from the bottom of your aunt, then you must expect . . . the unexpected.

Hugh gives up and smashes the door down.
Wendy, played by Caroline, appears worriedly in the hallway.

Caroline	Darling! What . . .?
Hugh	Jesus suffering ARSE! That bloody door.
Caroline	I don't understand.
Hugh	Don't understand? Don't understand? What's to understand, you hopeless saucer of pus? It's a frig-mothering door and it keeps getting vomiting stuck. That's all there is to understand. It's not differential calculus.
Caroline	Andrew!

Hugh heaves a colossal punch at her and sends her flying through the banisters which collapse satisfactorily. She lies in a dizzy heap.

Hugh	Now look what you've done, you pointless tart. You've broken the snotting bannisters.
Caroline	Andrew . . . is something wrong?

Hugh tuts violently and drops the flowers on her.

Hugh	I'm going to get myself a drink. Happy birthday, you saggy old bitch.

He storms off. Caroline looks at the flowers that have dropped on to her chest.

Caroline	They're lovely, darling. Thank you. And they . . . *(inhaling deeply)* . . . they smell gorgeous.

She takes another sniff. Cut to Hugh in the drawing room, pouring himself a drink. The lid on the whisky bottle is tight. This narks Hugh.

Hugh	Oh, come on. OPEN, you scrotuming dribble of faeces.

The lid opens.

That's better. *(Drinks)* Oh, that's much better.

Hugh looks at the drink and starts to smile.

Hugh	Only a door, after all. Not the end of the world. Silly to get all annoyed about . . .

His thoughts are cut off. Wendy suddenly throws an enormous punch at him, sending him miles across the room.

	What the . . .?
Caroline	Sorry.
Hugh	Sorry?
Caroline	Yes. Sorry I didn't hit you with a sockful of gravel, you flabby, drivelling, waste of clothes.
Hugh	Wendy, darling . . .
Caroline	'Wendy, darling'. I'll darling your arse with a rusty lawn-sprinkler . . .

She punches Hugh again. He gets up, holding his nose.

Hugh	What . . . what's happened?
Caroline	Happened? Nothing's happened that a Swiss Army penknife can't sort out. Now why don't you take these bottom-wipingly ugly flowers and stick them into your lungs?

Caroline tosses the flowers at Hugh, who looks at them.

Hugh	The flowers . . . flowers, that's it . . . Wendy, listen . . . I think I know what's happened. What this is all about.

Hugh starts to talk as Stephen's voice comes over. During this, Hugh gets up and starts drawing diagrams on a blackboard to explain his tale.

Stephen	And so, Wendy Beckett sat at her husband's knees and listened to a story. A fantastic story. A tale that danced along the crumbling brim of credibility, yet never once lost its footing. A tale of walking home, and pavements, and forgettings of birthdays, and rememberings, and wantings to buy flowerings, and discoverings of a flower-stall just at the right momentings. And when he was finished, Andrew Beckett took his young wife's face in his hands . . .
Hugh	Now do you understand, Wendy? Do you see what this is all about?
Caroline	Oh Andy. I feel such a fool.
Hugh	I think we've both been a little mad, Wendy. It's not a question of blame. What matters now is us. The future.
Caroline	Oh Andy . . .
Hugh	Oh Wendy . . .

As they embrace, the camera starts to pan off on to the waste-paper basket.

Stephen	A happy ending, you may think. Loose ends tied up, the books balanced. And yet ... and yet ... what of our friend the blind flower-seller?

Cut to Patrick selling to another passer-by.

Patrick	Old Man's Wrinkle, madam. Otherwise known as the Fighting Buttercup. They do say that the smell of these flowers brings out all the anger in a person ...
Passer-by	Really?
Patrick	And then, when they've done that for a bit ... they explode.

There is the sound of a distant explosion, and after a few seconds, a tinkle of broken glass and falling debris. The passer-by doesn't seem to notice.

Passer-by	How much?
Patrick	To you, madam, nothing.
Passer-by	Oh. Thanks very much.

She takes them and sniffs deeply. Close-up on Patrick as he starts to cackle fiendishly. We get closer and closer as his laugh gets louder and louder until suddenly, a fist knocks him out of view.
Cut to Stephen in his chair.

Stephen	Sleep well. If you can ...

VOX POP

Hugh In the morning? Oh, I used to use one of those things that automatically pour you a cup of tea and make a horrid screeching noise in your ear. But she divorced me. Now I use a Goblin Teasmade.

Stephen *(as a woman)* Well, I'm aroused every morning by a very insistent cock.

Grand Prix

Footage of Formula One cars getting the chequered flag. A sweaty Hugh, as a racing driver, is being interviewed by Stephen. Distant sounds of engines and crowds.

Stephen Michael, you must be thrilled with that result. Take us through the race.

Hugh Yes, well, I was not very happy with the car ... we had a lot of problems, the car was not so good, I think, and ...

Stephen But you won, it's a great result, you must be very happy.

Hugh Well, we had a lot of problems with the car, and I was not so happy, it was very hard ...

Stephen Yes but you won ...

Hugh I won, yes, but there were many, many problems, and it was very hard, and difficult, and I was not happy at all with the car ...

Stephen But you did actually, can I get this straight, you did actually win the race?

Hugh With a lot of problems, yes, I won the race, but it was very hard ...

Stephen Leaving aside how hard it was, are you *happy* to have won the race?

Hugh Well, it was very difficult, you know ...

Stephen Yes, presumably it was. Presumably, that's why you get paid half a million pounds per race and get as much sex as you can eat. My point is, that HAVING won it ... you must be very *HAPPY*. Pleased. Excited. Enchanté. Over the frigging moon.

Hugh Well, we had a lot of problems ...

Stephen ARE ... YOU ... HAPPY?

Hugh Many problems ...

Stephen ARE ... YOU ... HAPPY?

Hugh It was very hard ...

Stephen ARE ... YOU ... HAPPY?

Hugh Difficult ...

Stephen ARE ... YOU ... HAPPY?

Hugh Proble ...

Stephen ARE ... YOU ... ARSING WELL HAPPY, YOU DISMAL, MOANING, FRENCH TWAT?

Hugh What?

Stephen You do a job that half of mankind would kill to be able to do, you can go to bed with the other half any time you like, you are richer than Croesus, I just need to know if this makes you *HAPPY?*

Pause.

Hugh We had a lot of problems ...

Stephen lunges forward and punches Hugh full in the face.

Tribunal

Stephen M. and Phyllida sit behind a kind of bench as for a tribunal of some kind. Stephen, rat-faced and moustached, is up before them.

Phyllida	You are Councillor Kenneth Wade?
Stephen	I am.
Stephen M.	I hope you are aware, Councillor Wade, that this is an informal hearing?
Stephen	Indeed. I would like it understood at the outset that I have done nothing of which I am ashamed and that I stand by my record in local government. Having said that I am very happy to co-operate fully with this enquiry and answer such questions as might be put.
Phyllida	You were elected to Grangely City Council, Mr Wade, on a ticket of . . . let me see . . .
Stephen	. . . on a ticket of providing value for money for our charge-paying customers and injecting new standards of decency, honour and family values into the community.
Stephen M.	Fine words, no doubt, Mr Wade. You were, I believe, in charge of the 'contracting out' of the Council's cleaning services?
Stephen	Cleansing.
Stephen M.	I beg your pardon?
Stephen	Cleansing services. We call them cleansing services, not cleaning services.
Phyllida	Why?
Stephen	Um . . . because it annoys people, I suppose.
Stephen M.	And the company you contracted those cleansing services out to was called Wade Cleaning Ltd.
Stephen	Cleansing. Wade Cleansing. Slogan: we know the Meansing of Cleansing.
Phyllida	Wade Cleansing is wholly owned and run by your wife.
Stephen	The matter has already been fully investigated by an independent enquiry . . .
Stephen M.	Yes. Wade Independent Tribunals Ltd.
Stephen	Certainly. The old publicly-run enquiry procedures were expensive and inefficient, we contracted out to Wade Independent Tribunals Ltd, who offered a competitive, hard-headed, business-oriented tribunal and enquiry service.
Stephen M.	But which is wholly owned and run by your son, Geoffrey.
Stephen	As it happens, yes.
Stephen M.	Who is five months old.
Stephen	Five and a half months old. Geoffrey put together a very attractive bid. I was proud of him.
Stephen M.	Mm. Geoffrey's mother, however, is not your wife, but Miss Valerie Jephcott, your secretary.

Stephen	Yes. The sexual service my wife was offering was old-fashioned, inefficient, unwieldly and . . . after my older children's birth . . . overstretched and with a tendency to too much waste. I decided to contract out my sexual requirements, open them for competitive tender in the market-place. Valerie offered a sexual service that was faster, tighter, more efficient, more imaginative and more slimmed down than my wife's.
Phyllida	I thought you stood for family values and clean living?
Stephen	Cleanse living.
Phyllida	Cleanse living. In your electoral literature, for instance, you promised to come down hard on homosexuals.
Stephen	Since I've been in office I have spent a lot of money and energy coming down very hard indeed on homosexuals.
Stephen M.	To return to financial matters, Mr Wade. Do you think it is appropriate that in these very lean times for . . .
Stephen	In these very *lens* times . . .
Stephen M.	Whatever. The point is, you have been accused of making a lot of money from being a councillor.
Stephen	Yes. Well. There you have it: 'accused'. That's the attitude I have to deal with all the time. Making money is a crime, something to apologise for. Well, I'm sorry but when I grew up 'profit' wasn't a dirty word. '*Arse*' was a dirty word. 'Profit' wasn't. 'Scrotum' was a pretty dirty word too and so was 'titty'. Well, I'm not ashamed to say that I've never been afraid of hard graft, sheer bloody graft . . . or is 'graft' a dirty word too, like 'botty' and 'helmet'?
Stephen M.	I think we've heard enough, Councillor. This may be an informal hearing, but frankly, I'm sure we're agreed . . .

He cocks his head at Phyllida.

Phyllida	No quarrels. It's all there.
Stephen M.	Yes. Yes. Uh-huh. Good. *(To Stephen, solemnly.)* Kenneth Wade. Your name will now go forward as that of our officially adopted Parliamentary Candidate for the Grangely Constituency. *(Smiles.)* Congratulations, Ken.

Stephen comes up for a handshake. We see for the first time that we are in the Meeting Room of the Grangely Conservative Constituency HQ.

Stephen M.	Long live Britain.
Stephen	God Save the Quense.

Honda

Hugh is in the studio.

Hugh   Bit of a surprise piece of news here. We don't normally carry news stories, but this one does seem fairly major, and it would be silly to ignore it. According to a Reuters news flash, the British Government has apparently just been bought by Honda. The deal went through in the early hours of this morning, and has just been announced by Honda's Group Managing Director, Ralph Tokana. According to Reuters, Honda fought off rival bids from Unilever and the John Lewis Group, and is believed to have paid upwards of four hundred million for the troubled democracy giant. I think we have some footage here . . .

Cut to Stephen emerging from a Whitehall building. Cameras and flash bulbs. Hugh in voice-over.

. . . of . . . yes, that's Nigel Pargitter, no relation, Deputy Director of the Board of Trade . . .

Stephen   . . . we believe, very firmly, that this was a fair price, and that the British taxpayer has got a good deal here. Honda . . . may I just finish here? Honda have given us satisfactory undertakings to the effect that they will not be making any massive changes to the structure of government for at least six months, and that their only social alterations will involve converting Wales into a seven-million-hole golf course, and replacing all the houses and flats in Britain with perspex living-pods.

Stephen M.   Have you tried . . .?

Stephen   Yes, I've tried one of these pods myself, and it was very . . .

Phyllida   What about unemployment?

Stephen   Oh what *about* unemployment? You people, you're obsessed . . . every time some change comes along, some new idea that might really do this country a bit of good, it's the same old 'What about unemployment?' I mean, change the bleeding record, can't you? Yes, there will be some unemployment. Honda have pointed out that we really don't need 620 people in the House of Commons, for instance. They will be investing in a new, laser-guided legislative machine . . .

Stephen M.   So there will be no elected body?

Stephen   Oh come on! Just rejoice, can't you? It's a compliment: it shows that this government, as we've always claimed, is an attractive proposition to our customers. This is a good deal for Britain, a good deal . . .

Cut back to the studio.

Hugh   Well, I think I ought to say at this point, that that was all made up. Honda haven't really bought the British Government. It's a completely silly idea.

He gets up and runs over to a camera and looms into the lens.

Or is it?

VOX POP Hugh I said to the Captain, I said you want to watch out for those icebergs, because a lot of them are a lot bigger under the water than they look on top of the water, but no, he just had to plough on, showing off to all the women, so then, obviously, wallop. Big hole in the side, went down in under ten minutes. Egg on his face, I say.

Pooch

Hugh and Stephen are sitting in a vet's surgery waiting-room. Stephen has a long-haired dachshund on a lead. Hugh has a basket by him. Stephen's character is perfectly horrible in its tweeness.

Stephen	Wot'cha-got in there, I wonder?
Hugh	Cat.
Stephen	Got a mogs in there, have you? A kitti-puss? Lovely. This is Clover, my daxie. I've always had daxies. I like daxies with long coaties.
Hugh	Do you, do you, really? Is that right?
Stephen	What sort of mog-wog is your pussy-kit? A tabbles, a tom-tom or what?
Hugh	Burmese.
Stephen	A Burmie! I love a Burmie. Boy or girl Burmie?
Hugh	Oh God . . . male.
Stephen	*(into basket)* Hello, Mr Burmie. What's your name?
Hugh	Yes, it can't speak actually.
Stephen	Oh, but they can understand every word, can't they?
Hugh	Not much evidence for that.
Stephen	My first dax, my first little dax was called Sculley. I named him after Hugh Sculley from the *Antiques Roadshow*. I love that programme, don't you?
Hugh	Pevertedly.
Stephen	Do you know what I do of a Sunday? After I've taken Clover for walkums . . . we go walkums after lunch, don't we Clover . . . just Clover and me and of course my little pooper-scooper, because that nasty Parkie man doesn't like to see poochie-poop on his best grass, does he?
Hugh	Oh Christ . . .
Stephen	We come back and I make myself a cheese and tommy-toe toastie.
Hugh	Cheese and *what*?
Stephen	Tommy-toe. Tommy-toe. Tommy-toe.
Hugh	Tomato.
Stephen	Tommy-toe. Tommy-toe.
Hugh	Don't say it again.
Stephen	I make myself a cheese and tommy-toe toastie, sometimes two toasties, and a lovely old muggles of tea and I snudget down in time for the Roadshow. I love Sunday afternoonies.
Hugh	Jesus Christ oh help.
Stephen	If it's not the Roadshow, they have the animal programme with Desmond.
Hugh	Desmond Morris.
Stephen	We just call him Desmond in our house, cos he's like a friend. An old

	chum. Or there's *Masterchef* or the Clothsies Show. Clover and I love our Sunday afties, don't we Clover?
Hugh	Mmmmmmmmmmmmmmmmmmm.
Stephen	So what's wrong with Mr Burmie?
Hugh	What?
Stephen	Mr Burmie. Why's he come to see Vettiloo? Got a poorly tums?
Hugh	Did you just say Vettiloo?
Stephen	Sore throatie? *(Into basket.)* What's wrong with Mr Burmie?
Hugh	I've brought him in to be killed.
Stephen	Scusie?
Hugh	He's got cancer of the liver, so I've brought him in to be put to death.

A pause.

Stephen	Cancer?
Hugh	Yes.
Stephen	Cancer of the liver?
Hugh	Yes.
Stephen	Cancey-wancey.
Hugh	Oh Jesus . . .
Stephen	*(to the cat)* Cancey-diddlies. They going to put you to deathies, Mister Burmie? They going to stop your heartipoos from going beaty-weat-weat? Are they going to go killichum-chums? Put your coldy-woldy body-wods in a holey-ploppy-poo-woo?

The door to the vet's office opens and Phyllida pops her head round.

Phyllida	Clover?
Dachsund	*(looking up)* Yeah?
Phyllida	What can I do for you?
Dachsund	*(looking at Stephen)* I'd like to have him put down, please. As soon as possible.

Disgusting

Stephen I hate you, I despise you, I loathe you. Everything about you DISGUSTS me. Your ears, eyes, nose, mouth, tongue, legs, knees, stomach, ribs and bottom make me want to vomit up. You're repulsive, loathsome, grotesque and insupportable. I want to kill you. I want to twist your nipples off and throw them to the dogs. You scum. You low, corrosive lump of fecal horror, you maniac bastardly turd. I would rather drink stale urine from Norman Fowler's arse-pit than remain one moment more in your defiling company. You're filth, you're cack, you're the ooze of a burst boil, I abominate you, you towering mound of corrupted slime. Your every utterance is like the slithering hiss of a fat maggot in the putrid guts of a decomposing rat, your face is fouler than the unwiped inner ring of Satan's rectum.

Camera widens to show the sweetest, whitest-haired old granny ever seen. She pushes a cream cake towards Stephen.

Granny Have a cream slice, dear.
Stephen Thanks.

VOX POP **Hugh** I went on one of these wild man weekends. You know, reclaim one's nature, discover the innate masculinity inside me, confront the demons and angels of manhood in a wild, untrammelled journey of the soul. Bloody nearly froze to death.

Dalliard: Models

Stephen is there. Hugh enters.

Hugh	Good morning.
Stephen	I beg your pardon?
Hugh	I said good morning.

Stephen stands back, ashen-faced.

Stephen	At last . . .
Hugh	What?
Stephen	After all these years . . .
Hugh	Sorry . . .?
Stephen	Welcome, comrade. Welcome. Sit down. Rest your weary elbows. You'll take a glass of vodka? *(Calling.)* Mr Dalliard! Break out the false passports and the rabbit-skin hats. We are going to Moscow.
Hugh	Moscow?
Stephen	What news? Comrade Stalin in rude health, I trust?
Hugh	I'm sorry. I'm not with you. All I said was 'good morning'.
Stephen	Precisely. The code.
Hugh	Code?
Stephen	It is now twenty-seven summers since Comrade Molenski stood slightly to the left of where you are now and told me that, one day, a man would come into this shop and give notice of his allegiance with the phrase 'good morning'. And that, on hearing these words, Mr Dalliard and I were to detonate our relatives and fly to Dover.
Hugh	Fly to Dover?
Stephen	Where a man called Smith would see us safely on to a goods train carrying livestock to Minsk.
Hugh	Wait a minute. When I said 'good morning', all I meant was . . . good morning.
Stephen	Oh.
Hugh	I mean . . . that's all I meant.
Stephen	Ah. In that case, please accept my green felt apologies, and allow me to sing the fourth verse of 'An English Country Garden' omitting the line 'Where tom tits dwell' by way of recompense.
Hugh	No, really, don't bother . . .
Stephen	Are you quite sure, sir? Mr Dalliard will be happy to accompany me on his knees.
Hugh	Knees?
Stephen	Yes, sir. One of the most accomplished knee-players in this shop, is Mr Dalliard.

Hugh	No, that's alright. I just came in here to buy a model.
Stephen	A model?
Hugh	Yes.
Stephen	A model?
Hugh	Yes.
Stephen	A model?
Hugh	Yes.

Pause.

Stephen	A model?
Hugh	That's right. I want to buy a model.
Stephen	With or without plastic struts?
Hugh	Um ... I'm not really sure. I thought an aeroplane ...
Stephen	Let me ask a different question in the same way. Who is this model for?
Hugh	It's for my son.
Stephen	Your son?
Hugh	Yes.
Stephen	Just your son?
Hugh	Yes.
Stephen	And when is this 'birthday' of his?
Hugh	Wednesday.
Stephen	Yes, that's what I said. When's the day?
Hugh	Wednesday.
Stephen	Are you stupid or just plain deaf?
Hugh	Wednesday.
Stephen	*(overcome with embarrassment)* Oh, you are genuinely stupid. I'm so sorry. I thought you were just being deaf. Mr Dalliard, command the earth to swallow me up. I'm so sorry, life must be hard enough for stupid people without tactless old bastards like that lady over there rubbing it in with salt in your face widely. Mr Dalliard, I've gone peculiar.

Hugh looks round.

Hugh	What lady?
Stephen	So. In plain-flavoured English. When ... is ... your ... son's birthday?
Hugh	W ... the day after Tuesday.
Stephen	The day after Tuesday. Doctors are so specific these days, aren't they? And are you expecting him to be a boy or a girl?
Hugh	It's my son. He's nine. It'll be his tenth birthday.
Stephen	His tenth? Sir, you're spoiling him. I was only ever allowed one. On my birthday, usually. However. No doubt you know your own business best. Just don't come bleating to Mr Dalliard and me if this over-indulged child grows up to be one of those drug jockeys that

	you're always reading about on television. A glass of water?
Hugh	No thank you.
Stephen	A cup of water?
Hugh	No.
Stephen	A plate of water, then?
Hugh	Thank you, no. Just a model aeroplane.
Stephen	A *model aeroplane* of water?
Hugh	No. Forget the water. I don't want any water. Just the model aeroplane kit. I thought perhaps that Messerschmitt 109E in the window.
Stephen	The Messerschmitt 109E in the window.
Hugh	Yes please.
Stephen	*(with his hand on his head)* Fizzy or still?
Hugh	What?
Stephen	That doesn't count. I had my hand on my head. You must ignore anything I say with my hand on my head.
Hugh	Oh.
Stephen	So, the Messerschmitt 109E. Sir has a wonderful eye.
Hugh	Thank you.
Stephen	So blue. The ear is a disappointment. Not blue at all. I have a little tin of Humbrol paint in cobalt blue ... perhaps you would allow me to ...?
Hugh	No thank you. Just the model and I suppose some glue.
Stephen	Oh dear. Glue. So your son is already a drug jockey. Mr Dalliard and I warned you on bended legs, but would you listen? No. And now look at him.

Stephen gets from under the counter a beautifully finished and painted model of a Messerschmitt and a plastic bag with glue smeared inside it.

Hugh	What's this?
Stephen	A Messerschmitt 109E and a fix for your degenerate junkie of a son, sir.
Hugh	But the model's done.
Stephen	Sir?
Hugh	It's ready-assembled.
Stephen	You can't expect us to do all the work ourselves, sir. The whole joy of modelling lies in carefully scraping off the paint, soaking off the transfers and taking the plane apart piece by piece, and putting each of the pieces into a little plastic bag which is then sealed and placed inside the box. Something to be proud of. An achievement. Strange words in these days of Supersonic Hedgehog brothers and ready-sliced golf shots.
Hugh	Alright. Forget it. Just forget it. I'll go somewhere else.
Stephen	Mr Dalliard has a gun trained on you through the curtains. If you take so much as one step towards that door, sir, he will, at a word

	from me, shoot you clean through the head with as much pity as if you were a helpless seal-pup called Arnold.
Hugh	WHAT?

Stephen indicates to show that his hand is on his head.

Stephen	So sorry that we couldn't help you, sir. We try to accommodate our customers, but not being a hotel we find it almost impossible.
Hugh	Yes. Well. This hasn't been a very good morning.
Stephen	Good morning! Mr Dalliard! We have been activated. After all these years.

VOX POP **Hugh** You know that historian, David Irving? He doesn't exist. Completely made up.

Oprah Winfrey

Stephen addresses the camera in his normal clobber.

Stephen   Hello, I'm Oprah Winfrey. Today we're looking at self-esteem, what is it, do we have enough, where can we get more if we need it? With me is Louella Della Twee, author of *I Think I'm Great: Why Don't You?*

Cut wider to include Hugh, lolling in a chair in extravagant garb.

Louella, first of all, have you got self-esteem?

Hugh   No. I don't have it. Don't ask me why.

Stephen   Oh. Alright.

Hugh   God knows I should have it.

Stephen   Really?

Hugh   I'm an intelligent, beautiful, warm, loving, funny, sexy, rich, almighty heap of woman. The only thing I don't have is self-esteem.

Stephen   That's a bugger, isn't it? Now your book contains several uses of the word 'me'.

Hugh   I would agree with that.

Stephen   If . . .?

Hugh   If what?

Stephen   You would agree with that if . . .?

Hugh   If I had enough self-esteem.

Stephen   I see. No, what I was going to say was the first chapter contains nothing but the word 'me'. You have written the word 'me' 3,416 times.

Hugh   Seventeen.

Stephen   Is it?

Hugh   The chapter is called 'me'.

Stephen   So it is. Now, can I ask you this question. Why?

Hugh   Why me?

Stephen   Precisely.

Hugh   I don't love myself any more. I used to love myself when I was a kid, but then I stopped. I stopped talking to myself, seeing myself for what I really am. I took myself for granted.

Stephen   Let's have a pointless round of applause there.

Applause.

So what did you do?

Hugh   I confronted myself. I waited till I got home one day, and I said to myself, what are you doing?

94

Stephen	How unbearably tense. And how did you answer yourself?
Hugh	I shifted around, started blaming all kinds of things, then eventually I had to admit to myself that yes, I was sleeping with someone else.
Stephen	Had you suspected this?
Hugh	I knew. I knew all along. I just didn't want to face it. It was the deceit. But then I realised that the only person I was really deceiving was myself.
Stephen	I don't think I've ever been more emotionally knotted-up than I am at this moment. Yes, madam?

Phyllida stands up in the audience.

Phyllida	I just wanted to ask Louella where she gets her strength from?
Stephen	Louella, lady wants to know where the mascara arse you get your strength from?
Hugh	Can I answer that with a question?
Stephen	Can she?
Phyllida	I'd like that.
Stephen	She'd like that.
Hugh	I want you to do something for me. I want you to stand in front of a mirror, take your clothes off, every shred . . .

Laughter from the audience.

Hey, no, I'm serious, why not? You're you. I want you to stand naked in front of that mirror and I want you to say 'I like me just the way I am. I like my fat hips, and my lisp and my whining aggression. I love the fact that I'm neurotic. I'm happy that I demand the world's respect without having to earn it. I'm me, I'm special, I'm kinda crazy about me just the way I am.' Would you do that for me?

Wild applause from the audience.
  Another woman gets up.

Woman	Can I ask Louella something with a question? I have high self-esteem. It's ruining my life. I'm the only person I know with high self-esteem. It's terrible. I feel like I'm missing out.
Hugh	Honey, you've just got to learn to lower your self-esteem. Try and make up some story about being maybe abused as a child. Pretend your husband doesn't appreciate how artistic and special and interesting you are. It'll come.

Applause.

Stephen	We've got a vomit break right now. Don't go away.

Religianto

Hugh is supervising the gathering of thirty or so six-year-olds.

Stephen   (*voice-over*) Tony Racklin is headmaster of Lannark Primary School in Thurlow. The school has eighty-four pupils, of mixed race, religion, gender and shoe size. So how does he deal with religious instruction at the school's morning assembly?

Hugh sits at the piano and plays. The children vaguely join in.

Hugh   We worship you oh God or Gods,
Whoever you may be,
We realise that you operate
Supernaturally,
We thank you for the birds and bees,
For creatures live or dead,
But if you actually don't exist,
Please ignore what we've just said,
Aaaaaaaaaa

Cut to Hugh in interview.

What I've tried to do, what we've tried to do, I should say, is develop a religious agenda that serves the needs of the kids in a real sense. You must understand that we have here Muslim kids, Hindu kids, Christian kids, Jewish kids, atheistic kids, agnostic kids. What they've all got in common is that they're all . . .

Stephen   Kids?

Hugh   Exactly. That's very important. And therefore, the religious package we offer must take account of all those different elements under the over-arching umbrella of basic caring.

Stephen, listening to this, turns out of shot and vomits quite noisily.

Stephen   Sorry . . . don't know what happened there . . . so how have you done that? How have you accommodated these different . . .

Hugh   What I've done, what *we've* done, I should say, is sweep away all the old divisions and invent a new religion.

Stephen   A new religion?

Hugh   That's right. It's a kind of religious Esperanto, if you like.

Stephen   Nope. Don't think I do . . .

Hugh   We've called this religion Lip Wip Wip Wip.

Stephen	Lip Wip Wip Wip. Now is that the name of the God...?
Hugh	There is no one, single God in Lip Wip Wip Wip.
Stephen	It's a pantheon, is it?
Hugh	I call it a committee of Gods. There are eight voting members and a non-executive chair who rotates every four years.
Stephen	So what form does the worship take? What do you actually worship?
Hugh	We worship air...
Stephen	Air, right...
Hugh	And flexible work-share schemes...
Stephen	Aha...
Hugh	And anything that has a rounded corner on it.
Stephen	Why rounded corners?
Hugh	Well, they're a very important symbol in Lip Wip Wip Wip. The kids here worship the one on the edge of the activity table in our art-room...

Close-up of worktop. Pull out to see kids chanting at it.

Stephen	And what do rounded corners symbolise in Lip Wip Wip?
Hugh	Er ... the roundedness of things generally. The fact that you're much less likely to hurt yourself on round things or get things snagged on them. We prefer them to have a stain-resistant wipe-free surface, ideally. Every Farkling we place large potato prints...
Stephen	Sorry, every Farkling?
Hugh	Yes. Farkling is our equivalent of, oh, Christmas, Ramadan, Passover ... what you will. It's our major festival. We have it at the beginning of January so that parents can take advantage of the January sales when buying presents. It's traditional on Farkling Eve to place potato-printed pictures on a rounded-cornered surface overnight.

We see kids doing so – looking frankly pissed off.

	Then, when the kids come down they find they've been marked out of ten by Parent Farkling.
Stephen	Parent Farkling?
Hugh	Yes ... a sort of Father Christmas figure, but eitherly gendered.
Stephen	And instead of leaving filled stockings or something similar, they mark a potato-print picture out of ten?
Hugh	Yes – but of course, traditionally, every kid always gets ten.
Stephen	Bloody hell. You say 'traditionally', how long in fact has Lip Wip Wip Wip been a religion?
Hugh	Well, the religion arose out of some very exciting discussions we had during a level two resource allocation module steering committee meeting that the trust held last week...

Stephen	It's alright, I'm controlling myself. So, would you say the religion has been a success so far?
Hugh	Well, I'll be as frank as I can. There *have* been problems, I'm afraid.
Stephen	Oh?
Hugh	Mm. Just yesterday one of the kids in Mrs Tremloe's 2acvaw.xp5 class, Tristram, formed a sect that decided to worship oblong surfaces.
Stephen	Oh dear.

Cut to Hugh, sitting on the desk in the class-room with a small child stretched out on a torturer's rack. Hugh gives a turn of the wheel.

Hugh	Now, come on Tris. I'm very disappointed. What are you?

Tris wails. Hugh turns the wheel again.

Tristram	I'm a heretic.
Hugh	That's better. So, kids. What do you reckon we should do about that? Any thoughts?
Kids	Burn him! Burn the heretic! Torch him!
Hugh	OK. That's agreed then. We'll burn you at the stake in the playground during break, Tris. Now. Anna. What's this about you being a witch?

Cut back to Hugh and Stephen.

Hugh	Early days yet, but we're hoping to iron out some of these teething snags pretty soon and get a permanent dungeon in the old chapel.

Consent

Robert and Jeanine are facing each other across a boardroom table. Hugh is at Jeanine's side, Stephen at Robert's. Stephen and Hugh are opening briefcases and setting up their stall.

Hugh	Right, Richard, are you going to start?
Stephen	Probably better if I start, Nick, yes. Thrash out the position in broad terms, so we all know where we stand.
Hugh	That's got to be the right course, Richard. Got to be.
Stephen	I think so, Nick, I really do.
Hugh	Go you on ahead.
Stephen	Position is that my client wishes, in very broad terms...
Hugh	Broad terms?
Stephen	At this stage broad terms, yes, we can talk specifics later, my client wishes to engage in a protracted bout of sexual intercourse with your client.
Hugh	Can I chip in here, Richard?
Stephen	Chip in, chip in...
Hugh	Might save us a lot of time if I just say that my client is willing to consider your client's position in a favourable light, as long as we can thrash out some of the nitty-gritty.
Stephen	Oh, that's good news.
Hugh	So, shall we pencil a meeting, Richard, or...
Stephen	We could pencil a meeting, certainly, Nick, but I should say that my client is anxious to expedite matters and bring them to a speedy conclusion if at all possible.
Hugh	How speedy, Richard?

Stephen turns and mutters to Richard.

Stephen	My client was thinking along the lines of the next half-hour, Nick. I don't know how that sounds...
Hugh	Ah.

Hugh confers with Jeanine.

	My client, Richard, would like it clearly understood that she's not easy.
Stephen	My client clearly understands that your client is not easy, Nick, in fact he wishes me to stress that he has an enormous respect for your client in a variety of personal, non-sexual ways.
Hugh	My client is reassured by your client's position, and would like to know how your client intends to proceed.

Stephen and Robert mutter.

Stephen My client was thinking in general terms of dinner at the Bombay Brasserie, after which, at some mutually agreeable time, he would place his tongue inside your client's mouth and move it around slightly.

Hugh and Jeanine confer.

Hugh That is broadly acceptable to my client.

Stephen My client then suggests putting one of his hands up your client's skirt and having a bit of a feel.

Hugh Which hand, Richard?

Stephen My client hasn't yet decided which hand ...

Hugh Well perhaps you could fax us with that ...

Stephen Certainly, that's no bother ...

He makes a note.

'Fax Nick ... Which ... hand ... up ... skirt ...'

Hugh and Jeanine have been conferring.

Hugh I should say that after your client has put his hand up my client's skirt, my client reserves the right to moan slightly.

Stephen I don't see a problem there ...?

Robert shakes his head.

Stephen No, that's fine.

Hugh At this point, my client will suggest that your client drives my client back to your client's flat, where your client will play some James Taylor.

Stephen and Robert mutter.

Stephen My client doesn't have any James Taylor at the moment, and wonders whether Art Garfunkel would be acceptable?

Jeanine scribbles a note and pushes it across to Hugh.

Hugh Ah. My client insists that Art Garfunkel is definitely not acceptable, but would be prepared to consider Tom Waits.

Robert nods.

Stephen	Excellent. Moving on, my client would now like to insert . . .

Robert whispers something.

	Would now like to insert a clause allowing him to spill wine on your client's blouse and to mop it gently with a handkerchief, lightly brushing your client's breasts as he does so.
Hugh	We feel, in the interests of both parties, that a white wine spritzer should be specified.

Robert nods.

Stephen	A white wine spritzer it is. Now my client is keen to know whether your client can accommodate . . . (*Robert whispers.*)
Hugh	Yes?
Stephen	My client is keen to know whether your client can accommodate a circular licking motion around the upper body area at this stage.
Hugh	Perfectly acceptable. My client will be permitted to gaze at the ceiling and say the words 'Oh God' and 'Yes.'

Stephen writes down and mouths 'Oh God' and 'Yes' as Robert nods briskly.

Stephen	A move to the bedroom is now indicated.
Hugh	Indeed, I should point out, however, that my client is keen that this engagement should run along orthodox lines from hereonin.
Stephen	Would that preclude the use of salad items?

Firm nod from Jeanine.

Hugh	I'm afraid so.

Robert slightly disappointed.

Stephen	My client believes in that case that things can be satisfactorily brought to a conclusion in three minutes, after which time . . .
Hugh	My client feels that this would be premature. Ten minutes is more acceptable.

Robert looks aghast and swallows slightly.

Stephen	Shall we compromise with six?
Hugh	Six minutes then. I assume your client will then roll over and turn his back on my client?
Stephen	My client will most certainly do so. Your client will attempt to hold

	him and he will behave coldly.
Hugh	Quite so. My client will feel spurned and shamed as your client refuses to share the afterglow.
Stephen	My client then plans to sneak into his clothes at five in the morning and go very early to work, leaving no note for your client.
Hugh	My client will feel immensely rejected and angry at this.
Stephen	Quite so. My client will pick up the phone once during the afternoon, but fail to go through with calling, after which time he will not be in touch again.
Hugh	My client will from hereonin refer to your client as 'that bastard'.
Stephen	My client will blush and look away if ever he sees your client at a party.
Hugh	Precisely so. I think that's all satisfactory.

Robert and Jeanine both nod. Robert looks guilty, Jeanine looks cross.

Stephen	If your client will sign here . . .

Passes over contract.

Hugh	And yours here . . .

They each sign.

	Excellent.
Stephen	First-rate.

Robert and Jeanine stand. From across the table Jeanine slaps Robert in the face.

Jeanine	Bastard.

She storms out. Robert shuffles out through the other door.

Hugh	Marvellous.
Stephen	Splendid.

Pause.

Hugh	Fancy a quick shag?
Stephen	Oh alright.

Truancy

A bedroom. Hugh is playing a video game, sullen teenager-wise. Stephen enters.

Stephen	Terry. Got a moment?
Hugh	What?
Stephen	Do you have a window in your packed schedule? If so, could you open the curtains and let me look through? Just for a moment.
Hugh	Yeah.
Stephen	Good. Now Terry. School. I've had Mr Stroke on the phone, asking where you've been. He says you didn't turn up today.
Hugh	So?
Stephen	So why not?
Hugh	'S boring.
Stephen	How would you know that, Terry? According to Mr Stroke, you haven't been to school for nearly four years.
Hugh	So?
Stephen	So? So? So? So what have you been doing? What the hell have you been doing for the last four years?
Hugh	I've got to level nine.
Stephen	Level nine? What do you mean, level nine?
Hugh	Level nine. Top level.
Stephen	But school, Terry. Improvement. Learning. Discovery. Growth.
Hugh	What's the point?
Stephen	What's the point? What do you mean, what's the point?
Hugh	There's no point.
Stephen	There doesn't have to be a point, you blithering twerp. School is school. What's the point of ear lobes? What's the point of fabric conditioner, or tag wrestling, or butterfly-shaped pasta?
Hugh	School's boring.
Stephen	Yes? Your point being?
Hugh	I don't want to go to school, cos it's boring.
Stephen	You don't want? You don't want? And who, please be good enough to tell me, is supposed to give an electrically operated shag about what you want? Hmm? Hmmm? Hmmmmm?

A telephone rings. Neither Hugh nor Stephen takes any notice.

Hugh	Just leave me alone, can't you?
Stephen	Leave you alone? Leave you alone? Why the hell should I leave you alone? Are you making a cheese sauce? Working on a cure for cancer?

	An oboe concerto is starting to take shape in your mind? What?
Hugh	I'm on level nine.
Stephen	Bugger level nine. Bugger up the arse of level nine with an anglepoise lamp. I'm talking about your life.
Hugh	What about it?
Stephen	Never mind what about it? What *is* it, Terry? What the hell is your life? Tell me what your life is.
Hugh	What's yours?
Stephen	What do you mean, what's mine?
Hugh	What's your life?
Stephen	My life. My life. My life is about work, dedication, energy. Thirty-three bloody years with Russell and Bromley, that's what. My life is about having you. I had you, didn't I? That was supposed to be a good thing.
Hugh	I didn't ask to be born.
Stephen	You didn't ask to be born. Judas Priest on a two-stroke moped . . . what is that supposed to mean? Hm? What does that mean, you didn't ask to be born? You'd rather be dead, would you?
Hugh	Maybe.
Stephen	Maybe? Maybe? Maybe? Maybe? I mean . . . what?
Hugh	I've thought about it.
Stephen	About killing yourself?
Hugh	Yeah.
Stephen	Well, what's stopped you? Couldn't be bothered, I suppose. Couldn't be bothered to go down to the kitchen and get a knife out of the drawer.
Hugh	I wanted to get to level nine.
Stephen	You've got to level nine, for crying out loud from the bloody roof-tops. You're at level nine now.
Hugh	Right.
Stephen	Right.
Hugh	So when I finish this game, I'm going to top myself.
Stephen	Oh great. As long as I know. I'll go and book the bloody headstone now then. 'Here lies Terry Gardner, he got to level bloody nine.' Care for some singing cherubs round it, or do you want it plain?
Hugh	Bingo. Done it.

Hugh throws down the video game.

Stephen	So. Knife, or out of the window.
Hugh	Knife, I think.
Stephen	Knife, good.

Hugh goes out. Stephen listens for a moment, then picks up the video game.

Stephen	About bloody time.

Death Threat

Stephen and Hugh are there.

Stephen Ladies and gentlemen, bit of a shadow has been cast over the show this week. Hugh has received a death threat.

Hugh That's right.

He holds up a letter.

I got this letter this morning, addressed to 'Dear Sir or Madam, you are a cow son bastard sucking mental, you die heavily in wet throat ripping everywhere, don't like the Queen this country, for tear out lungs and replace with portable clothes, brackets yes please brackets. National Service who is she, stripping scrotum through eary leery pastures of deep smell.' Pretty upsetting, as you can imagine.

Stephen *(taking the letter)* I've tried to persuade Hugh to take this threat seriously, but he insists on carrying on as if nothing had happened.

Hugh If you give in to these people then . . . you've given in.

Stephen At the very least, Hugh, I don't think it's safe for you to do your song tonight.

Hugh No. If I don't do the song then he's won and democracy might as well take an early shower.

Stephen But *(looking at the letter, trying to make out the handwriting)* this . . . whoever he is, this 'M. Pontillo' might be in the audience tonight, armed.

Hugh One has to make a stand.

Stephen I think we would all understand if we skipped your song tonight. This Pontillo is probably lurking in the piano, with a mobile rocket launcher. M'colleague, listen to me. YOU MUST NOT SING TONIGHT.

Hugh I know you mean well, m'colleague, but my face is made up. For evil to flourish it only needs the good man to spout clichés. I'm going on.

Hugh moves towards the singing area.

Stephen Ladies and gentleman, m'colleague will now bravely entertain us with a young song. *(Ripping up letter: sotto voce.)* Well, that's thirty pence postage and package down the drain.

All We Gotta Do

Hugh strums a guitar and blows a harmonica. Then ...

Hugh
The poor keep gettin' hungry,
The rich keep gettin' fat,
Politicians change,
But they're never gonn' change that,
But you an' me girl,
We got the answer right in our hands,
All we gotta do is ...

Mumbles feebly.

The winds of war are blowin'
And the tide is comin' in,
Don't you be hopin' for the good times,
Because the good times have already been,
But girl, we got the answer,
So easy you won't believe,
All we gotta do is ...

Mumbles.

It's so easy to see,
If only they'd listen to you and me,
We got to ...
As fast as we can,
We got to ...
Every woman every man,
We got to ...
Time after time,
We got to ...
... dka and lime ...

The world is gettin' weary,
And it wants to go to bed,
Everybody's dyin',
'Cept the ones that are already dead,
But girl, we got the answer,
It's starin' us right in the face
All we gotta do is ...

Long pause. Then he goes back to the opening harmonica riff. Fade out.

Fast Monologue

Stephen, in huge close-up, monologises at really quite ripsnortingly immense speed.

Stephen   When I was seventeen I had already tried fourteen different jobs, married twice, fathered many many many children, eaten a perfectly enormous quantity of food over a long time period, been weaned off six types of class A dangerous drugs, given up smoking, taken it up again, given it up again, taken it up again, given taking it up and taken giving it up again and again and again. By the time I was twenty, alcohol had never passed my lips, yet I was a reckless and predatory alcoholic: my life was in pieces, my marriages were shattered, my children lay in ruins, my coffee was tasting increasingly bitter, I was paying alimony along the sinuses, behind the dark interior passages of the skull and through the nose. Nothing smelt felt dealt me right. My friends, ha! Friends? Friends, more like. My friends shunned me as you might shun a cigarette lighter or a brown caravan. In my twenty-fourth year I had increasing problems coping with live music, I lost my sense of utterness, and all feeling and movement in both testicles. Testicles? Did I say testicles? Testicles, more like. Rashes came and went: more wives, more children. My first daughter was severalteen by this time and inclined to chat. Nothing, nothing had prepared me for this. Life, they call it. Life? Life? Life? A living life, I called it. Desire, mood, memory, heat, sweat, effort, power, diction and a great quadratic equation of violent wanting, needing and rinsing. Words tumbled from me then as I knew that the answer lay, not in poetry, not in music, art, sculpture, drama, dance or investment analysis. The answer lay in a new way. A new way on. Some infection gripped me by the kidneys and said 'a new way, Randall, a new way'. So still barely twenty-five and three-quarters I rode that mountain, I trod that vineyard, I slept that great sleep of destiny, I danced to that music of memory and pogoed my soul to the insane rhythms of the heart's mind's vapid texture of journeys. Journeys? Gurneys more like. No, journeys, I was right. Still the fat gathered to my sinews and the corpuscles sang in my veins. Answers? No answers: fate had dealt me a dog turd and I read it as a full house. No answers, just the dead chiming of those twin tomb-black, doom-muffled husbands of decay, Bitterness and Rice. But then, then: opportunity knocked once for no, twice for yes. The labial seam of lead-grey cloud opened its fiery slit and showed me one glimpse, one escape, one chance to cut and run and never look back, no not once, just run, dead-run, blind-run. Fortune shat gold and told me under whose pillow to hide it. No wives now, no children, they had all grown up, got married themselves, got safe oh-so-spittingly-secure jobs and retired to golf-villas in the Algarve with beige cardigans, Beefeater and slimline and heavily descended testicles. But at thirty, that chance, that chance to . . . is 'redeem' the right word? That chance to redeem a bin-liner of broken shards and sworn devices. If I didn't take that chance what would I be? What would I become? Just another friendless acid spot on the back buttock of a weeping society. So I took it, took the chance, picked up the ball and ran, went for it, threw caution to the teeth of the gale, never look back, just keep running, I did it. Forget the past, there's nothing there, not even memories, just a road you never travelled unwinding backwards to a place you never came from . . .

Hugh enters behind Stephen, looking worried.

. . . where fruit grows on trees you never climbed, in an orchard where you lost your virginity to a boy called Timothy who died of Horlicks poisoning before you were born. No answers there. I went on. I . . .

Hugh	Stephen?
Stephen	Yes?
Hugh	Lie down for a while.
Stephen	OK.

VOX POP Hugh *(as a woman)* I've got three. Amanda, Lucy and little Emma. Just the three: I'm a busy woman, I think three lesbian lovers is plenty.

Stapler

Stephen and Robert hover over a Whitehall desk. The door opens and Hugh enters.

Stephen	Peter. Glad you could join us. You know Admiral Farquharson, I believe.
Hugh	Admiral.
Robert	Good afternoon, Peter. How's the model coming along?
Hugh	Getting there.
Stephen	Model? Something I should know?
Robert	Last time Peter and I worked together, he was building a model.
Stephen	Really? What of?
Hugh	I'm making a box of matches out of bits of old warship.
Robert	Surprising, wouldn't you say? Man like that.
Stephen	I gave up being surprised by Peter Haggard a long time ago.

Stephen and Robert chuckle.

	Now then, Peter, I expect you're wondering what all this is about?
Hugh	With respect, Sir, I'm not paid to wonder. I'm paid to do.
Stephen	But one of the things you do, surely, is wonder. Isn't it?
Hugh	Wondering is a luxury I can't afford.
Stephen	Really?
Robert	May I, Sir Richard?
Stephen	Of course.
Robert	We have a problem, Peter. A sticky one.
Hugh	Is there another kind?
Stephen	Oh yes, I should say so ...
Robert	Sir Richard ...
Stephen	Sorry.

Robert opens a drawer and pulls out a stapler.

Robert	Ever seen one of these before, Peter?
Hugh	A stapler.
Robert	Yes?

Hugh picks up the stapler and hefts it.

Hugh	Rexel Taurus. 56 half-inch staples. Comes in black, red or blue.
Stephen	Hah. I told you he was good.
Robert	No. I told *you* he was good.
Stephen	Did you?

Hugh	I assume there's a point to all of this?
Stephen	Oh there's a point, alright.
Robert	If it came to it, Peter, and I'm not saying it will, I'm saying *if*...
Hugh	Understood.
Robert	Do you think you could use one of these?
Hugh	You mean...?
Stephen	I think you know what the Admiral is saying, Peter. He's asking you whether you'd be prepared to staple two pieces of paper together.
Robert	If it came to it. And I'm not saying it will...
Stephen	He's not saying it will. He's saying *if*...

Hugh looks at the stapler.

Hugh	Been a long time.
Stephen	Been a long time for all of us, Peter. Too long, I sometimes think.
Hugh	And if I say no? Turn round and walk out of here, pretend none of this ever happened?
Robert	That is of course your right. Nobody is ordering you to do this thing.

Hugh chews his lip.

Stephen	What say you, Peter? Give it a go?
Hugh	And the pieces of paper? I'm not saying I'll do it, but *if*...
Robert	Sir Richard and I understand perfectly. Over there.

Robert points to a side table and Hugh picks up two pieces of paper. Robert is about to say something, but Stephen stops him.

Stephen	(sotto voce) If he does it, it'll be his decision. You don't push a man like Peter Haggard.
Robert	You're right, of course.

Hugh lines up the pieces of paper and picks up the stapler. He looks into the far distance. We superimpose shots of a woman running, explosions, laughing children, searchlights. Then come back to Hugh for a moment of indecision; he slides the stapler over the paper, grits his teeth and snaps it shut.

Stephen	Good man, Peter.
Robert	Thank you, Peter. That's not just from us. The nation thanks you.

Hugh smiles.

Hugh	Any time.

He goes out.

Robert   Thank God he's on our side.

VOX POP **Stephen** I have an old tape of Carlo Maria Giulini conducting the Vienna Philharmonic in a perfectly transcendent version of Schubert's seventh symphony. I've rigged it up so that at exactly half past seven every morning it falls from the ceiling on to my face.

Hugh *(as a woman)* I haven't got an alarm clock, I've got three children instead. It was a difficult choice, but I thought the children would go better with the wallpaper.

Time Complaint

Jeanine is behind the counter of a Dixons or similar enshoppment. Robert enters.

Jeanine	Good morning, sir.
Robert	Morning. I'd like to speak to someone about a refund, please.
Jeanine	Yes?
Robert	Yes.
Jeanine	Yes?
Robert	Oh I see. I have an appliance, bought from this shop, and it's sort of broken. So . . .
Jeanine	Oh dear. What is the appliance, sir?
Robert	It's a time machine.
Jeanine	A what?
Robert	A time machine. Panasonic. KL 500.
Jeanine	You bought a time machine in this shop, sir?
Robert	Well, I didn't. My niece did.
Jeanine	I see. When was this, sir?
Robert	July '97.
Jeanine	Right. And there's something wrong with it, is there?
Robert	Well yes, I set it to go back to October 5th 1970, because I wanted to see the last ever Janice Joplin concert, and it broke down. I don't know why . . .
Jeanine	You travelled back in time from 1997.
Robert	'98. I left it in its box for six months because I didn't have an adaptor.
Jeanine	Aha. Have you got the receipt?
Robert	'Fraid not. It was a present from . . .
Jeanine	Your niece, right. Has she got the receipt?
Robert	Doubt it. She hasn't been born yet.
Jeanine	Hhhmm. Tricky. Er . . . how much did she pay for this machine, if you don't mind me asking?
Robert	Will she pay?
Jeanine	Will she pay?
Robert	£99.99.
Jeanine	Cheap for a time machine.
Robert	Not if it doesn't work.
Jeanine	No, of course not. I'm going to talk to the manager, if you don't mind waiting.
Robert	Not at all.

Jeanine departs and Robert fiddles with gadgets: Jeanine comes back.

Jeanine	Good morning, sir.
Robert	Morning. I'd like to speak to someone about a refund, please.
Jeanine	Yes?
Robert	Yes.
Jeanine	Yes?
Robert	Oh I see. I have an appliance, bought from this shop . . . you see, it's done it again.
Jeanine	Done what again?
Robert	It's sticking. It keeps sticking, for some reason . . .
Jeanine	What does?
Robert	The time machine.
Jeanine	Time machine?
Robert	Yes. My niece is going to give me this time machine, but it's not going to work properly, so I'd like a refund.
Jeanine	Are you alright?
Robert	Perfectly. But the time machine keeps sticking, you see . . .
Jeanine	Are you alright?
Robert	Perfectly. But the time machine keeps sticking, you see . . .
Jeanine	Are you alright?
Robert	No, I'm insane.

VOX POP **Hugh** My favourite film? What's that one where Julia Roberts plays a convent-school fifth-former who comes round to my house and mistakes my face for a chair? Or did I make that one up?

Cocktails

Stephen addresses the camera while Hugh lets his fingers lightly dance on the keys of the old pianner.

Stephen	M'colleague, m'colleague . . . what a melancholy occasion is this.
Hugh	It is that, m'colleague. It is that. And yet . . .
Stephen	And yet?
Hugh	And yet for millions it is a time of simple rejoicing and quiet explosions of merriment.
Stephen	I hate you.
Hugh	I know what you're trying to say.
Stephen	But how, m'colleague, how shall I find fit words with which to bid an eternal farewell to our viewing several?
Hugh	Let go, Luke. Feel the force. Be in touch with your *feelings*.
Stephen	Yes . . . yes. O viewing several. Time . . . time, like a thief in the night has sneaked quietly up, smashed our near side window and ripped the stereo from our dashboard. Time, the fell predator, has stopped us in the underlit alleyway of circumstance, forced us to drop our trousers and had us up against the wall of eternity, grunting and sweating with degenerate, maniac pleasure. For the very last time I turn, wiping a sad soft salt tear from my crimsoning cheek as I request and require our disastrously lovely guest units to tell me what is and will be their choice of farewell cocktails, asking them only to tell me in words what their hearts cannot speak.

The guests confer.

Robert	*(to Jeanine: sotto)* I like the sound of a London Felch.
Jeanine	What about a Golden Shower?
Robert	Mm . . . good idea. We should be concentrating on choosing a cocktail first, though.
Jeanine	Yes . . .

They whisper.

Robert	There's the Martini Navratilova . . .
Jeanine	*(to Stephen)* What's a Sodding Mary?
Stephen	Like a Bloody Mary, but a little bit ruder. Have to hurry you . . .

They have decided.

Robert	Yes . . . you're right . . .

Jeanine	That's the one.
Both	We'd like a Modern Britain.
Stephen	A Modern Britain. Ha! M'colleague, what did you say to me only this morning?
Hugh	*(shaking his head)* What indeed.

Robert starts to play 'The Last Post' on a nearby trumpet, while Hugh and Jeanine lower a Union Jack with lashings of dignity.

Stephen   The cocktail you have chosen is Modern Britain. A Modern Britain is like the classical Old Fashioned, but with a new twist. For a Modern Britain, you'll need finely made English hand-blown crystal glasses, the very best Islay malt whisky, bred and lovingly blended by craftsmen who care: you'll need freshly squeezed apple juice from pleasant Somerset orchards, a quarter gill of London gin, a pint of rich Jersey cream, a half quart of soft, still Welsh mountain water, and to garnish, a shamrock, a daffodil, a thistle and a rose. To complete the Modern Britain we add to this kindly, noble, honourable and civilised mixture a centilitre of flat cola-style syrup, a hectare of low-cal brand sweetener, a pot of non-dairy whitener, a leisure-sachet of instant heritage, a two-parent family size pack of diluted good values, free-market vegetables, a greedy helping of self-governing trusts and a plastic ice-cube for cosmetic purposes only. The product should be half-baked at an immoderate temperature of the lowest common denominator in an atmosphere of greasy cant and corrupt sleaze, until richly dishonoured and seared with shame. Your Modern Britain will ideally have lost all colour, flavour and fizz by now and should then be divided against itself and left in shoddy disrepair for a number of years until it rots before being sold off to the highest bidder. An ideal self-serving suggestion would be to accompany the whole botched cocktail with a raft of unappetising sound-bites and a package of feeble initiatives stuffed with tasteless media slime. But perhaps, somewhere, you might be inspired to add one small, tender, caring cherry of hope. I wonder. While you decide, I will entreat for the very finalest of last, last times, this entreaty of m'colleague, Britain's own Melody Man as I say, 'Please, oh please, for all our sakes, please Mr Music, will you play?'

Hugh plays. Stephen mixes the cocktail.

Tutti   Soupy, soupy, soupy, soupy-soupytwist.